It's time for action.
COWS IN ACTION!

Genius cow Professor McMoo and
his trusty sidekicks, Pat and Bo,
are star agents of the C.I.A.
– short for COWS IN ACTION!
They travel through time, fighting
evil bulls from the future and
keeping history on the right track ...

Find out more at
www.**cows**in**action**.com

Read all the adventures of McMoo, Pat and Bo:

www.cowsinaction.com

Also by Steve Cole:

ASTROSAURS

Coming soon!

ASTROSAURS ACADEMY

www.astrosaurs.co.uk

THE VIKING EMOO-GENCY

Steve Cole

Illustrated by Woody Fox

RED FOX

THE VIKING EMOO-GENCY
A RED FOX BOOK 978 1 849 41401 2

First published in Great Britain by Red Fox,
an imprint of Random House Children's Books
A Random House Group Company

This edition published 2012

1 3 5 7 9 10 8 6 4 2

Text copyright © Steve Cole, 2012
Illustrations by Woody Fox, © Random House Children's Books 2012

The right of Steve Cole to be identified as the author
of this work has been asserted in accordance with
the Copyright, Designs and Patents Act 1988.

The Random House Group Limited supports the Forest Stewardship Council
(FSC®), the leading international forest-certification organization. Our books
carrying the FSC label are printed on FSC®-certified paper. FSC is the only
forest-certification scheme endorsed by the leading environmental organizations,
including Greenpeace. Our paper-procurement policy can be found at
www.randomhouse.co.uk/environment.

MIX
Paper from
responsible sources
FSC® C016897

Set in 16/20pt Bembo Schoolbook

Red Fox Books are published by Random House Children's Books,
61–63 Uxbridge Road, London W5 5SA

www.**kids**at**randomhouse**.co.uk
www.**randomhouse**.co.uk

Addresses for companies within The Random House Group Limited
can be found at: www.randomhouse.co.uk/offices.htm

THE RANDOM HOUSE GROUP
Limited Reg. No. 954009

A CIP catalogue record for this book is available
from the British Library.

Printed and bound by CPI Group (UK) Ltd, Croydon, CR0 4YY

For Victoria Charlotte Ready

★ THE C.I.A. FILES ★

Cows from the present –
Fighting in the past to protect the future . . .

In the year 2550, after thousands of years of being eaten and milked, cows finally live as equals with humans in their own country of Luckyburger. But a group of evil war-loving bulls — the Fed-up Bull Institute — is not satisfied.

Using time machines and deadly ter-moo-nator agents, the F.B.I. is trying to change Earth's history. These bulls plan to enslave all humans and put savage cows in charge of the planet. Their actions threaten to plunge all cowkind into cruel and cowardly chaos . . .

The C.I.A. was set up to stop them.

However, the best agents come not from 2550 — but from the present. From a time in the early 21st century, when the first clever cows began to appear. A time when a brainy bull named Angus McMoo invented the first time machine, little realizing he would soon become the F.B.I.'s number one enemy . . .

COWS OF COURAGE – TOP SECRET FILES

PROFESSOR ANGUS MCMOO

Security rating: Bravo Moo Zero

Stand-out features: Large white squares on coat, outstanding horns

Character: Scatterbrained, inventive, plucky and keen

Likes: Hot tea, history books, gadgets

Hates: Injustice, suffering, poor-quality tea bags

Ambition: To invent the electric sundial

LITTLE BO VINE

Security rating: For your cow pies only

Stand-out features: Luminous udder (colour varies)

Character: Tough, cheeky, ready-for-anything rebel

Likes: Fashion, chewing gum, self-defence classes

Hates: Bessie Barmer – the farmer's wife

Ambition: To run her own martial arts club for farmyard animals

PAT VINE

Security rating: Licence to fill (stomach with grass)

Stand-out features: Zigzags on coat

Character: Brave, loyal and practical

Likes: Solving problems, anything Professor McMoo does

Hates: Flies not easily swished by his tail

Ambition: To find a five-leaf clover – and to survive his dangerous missions!

Prof. McMoo's TIMELINE OF NOTABLE HISTORICAL EVENTS

13.7 billion years BC
BIG BANG - UNIVERSE BEGINS
(and first tea atoms created)

4.6 billion years BC
PLANET EARTH FORMS
(good job too)

23 million years BC
FIRST COWS APPEAR

(23 million is my lucky number!)

1700 BC
SHEN NUNG MAKES FIRST CUP OF TEA
(what a hero!)

7000 BC
FIRST CATTLE KEPT ON FARMS
(Not a great year for cows)

1901 AD
QUEEN VICTORIA DIES
(she was not a-moo-sed)

2550 BC
GREAT PYRAMID BUILT AT GIZA
(by an Egyptian geezer)

31 BC ROMAN EMPIRE FOUNDED

(Roam-Moo empire founded by a cow but no one remembers that)

1509 AD HENRY VIII COMES TO THE THRONE

(and probably squashes it)

1066 AD BATTLE OF HASTINGS

(but what about the Cattle of Hastings?)

1620 AD ENGLISH PILGRIMS SETTLE IN AMERICA

(bringing with them the first cows to moo in an American accent)

1939 AD WORLD WAR TWO BEGINS

(or World War Moo as it is known to cows)

2007 AD I INVENT A TIME MACHINE!!!

(about time!)

2500 AD COW NATION OF LUCKYBURGER FOUNDED

(HOORAY!)

2550 AD COWS IN ACTION RECRUIT PROFESSOR McMOO, PAT AND BO

(and now the fun REALLY starts…)

1903 AD FIRST TEABAGS INVENTED

THE VIKING
EMOO-GENCY

Chapter One

COWS MIGHT FLY!

As the sun's first stirrings warmed the skies over Farmer Barmer's organic farm – *CREEEAK!* – the door of a cowshed swung noisily open.

Pat Vine, a young, inquisitive bullock, peered out from inside. "All clear, Professor," he whispered.

"*Mooo*vellous!" The booming voice was deafening in the dawn quiet. "My latest invention's first ever test flight. Imagine that, Pat. I can't wait!"

Pat smiled as Professor Angus McMoo, a brilliantly brainy bull, moved out of his shed and into the thin morning light.

"Conditions are perfect!" McMoo

declared, slurping from a steaming-hot bucket of tea that fogged up his glasses. "Just enough light to see by and no wind." A rude bottom noise erupted from inside the shed. "Well, not *much* wind."

"Sorry, Prof!" came a higher voice from the shadows. "Just a bit nervous of trying out your new contraption."

"Oh, Little Bo," McMoo began, "if you're scared we can forget the whole—"

"SCARED? I don't do scared!" Little Bo Vine, Pat's big sister, stomped out of the shed – with a huge pair of feathered wings strapped to her back! "But what if this gadget of yours blows up? I'll be a flying barbecue!"

"You'll be fine,"

McMoo assured her. "The wings are powered by your heartbeat. *You* are the motor!"

"The *moo*tor, more like," Pat suggested. "Shame the wings aren't connected to your mouth, Bo – they'd send you into orbit!"

Bo scowled. "Watch it!"

"Shh, you two," said McMoo. "This invention could be very important to the C.I.A. in their fight against the F.B.I."

Pat nodded solemnly. Any humans listening in – assuming a) they understood cow language, and b) they hadn't run away screaming by now – might have thought McMoo was talking about America's Central Intelligence Agency and the Federal Bureau of Investigation having a scrap. But the truth of the matter was far stranger.

C.I.A. here stood for Cows In Action, a crack force of time-travelling cattle commandos – and McMoo, Pat and Bo were its star agents! All three belonged to a special breed of clever cows called Emmsy-Squares, and the F.B.I. they fought was the Fed-up Bull Institute – a menacing force from the far future who wanted evil cattle to conquer the world . . .

In the savage struggle to stop the cruel bulls, any advantage could be vital. McMoo had already invented the world's first time machine, disguised as an ordinary cowshed. Pat supposed that creating wings for a cow was a doddle.

"Switch on, Bo." McMoo grinned. "A two-minute test flight, then back to the shed for a cuppa."

Bo blew a gum-bubble and pressed a white button on the front of her harness. *Ba-dump! Ba-dump!* A noise like a heartbeat started up – and the wings began to flap! "It's working, Prof!" Slowly she rose into the air. "Woo-hoo-*mooo*!"

"Concentrate, Bo," McMoo urged her.

"You should be
able to control
your flight just by
thinking . . ."

Bo spiralled
improbably
through
the air,
cooing and
mooing.

"Wheee!"

"Keep the
noise down,"
McMoo hissed. "You
don't want to wake Bessie
Barmer!"

Pat shuddered. Farmer Barmer
was nice enough, but his wife Bessie
was big and smelly, and nastier than any
animal around. "Bo, look out – you're
flying too near the farmhouse!"

"Come off it, I'm miles away – *OOF!*"
There was an almighty *WHAM* as Bo
bumped against the wall and her udder
whacked an upper window.

Moments later, a woman's voice
bawled out: "WHAT WAS THAT?
SOMEONE CHUCKING STUFF
AT ME?"

"It's Bessie!" squealed Pat as McMoo
hauled him behind a bush for cover.
"Look out, Bo!"

But it was Bessie who was looking
out – or rather, *glowering* out – through
her bedroom window. She didn't realize
Bo was actually hovering just above
the roof! "If anyone's out there, they're
going to regret it . . ." The ugly woman
glared out a few seconds longer, then
stomped away.

Bo flapped back to the window and
pulled a rude face – just as a long lasso
was tossed out from behind the bushes
in the front garden! It looped round her

6

neck, and with a sudden
jerk she was yanked
down to the ground.

"Bo!" McMoo
jumped out of hiding.
"Quickly, Pat – she's
under attack!"

"Get off me!"
Bo yelled. There was
a ripping noise and the sound of a
hefty thump. Pat and McMoo raced over
and jumped the bushes like champion
racehorses . . .

To find a broken net and a fuming
Bo with wonky wings sitting on top of
a struggling, terrified bull. He wore a
black suit and sunglasses, and a small
pointy hat sat crumpled on his head.

"Try to catch me, would you?" Bo
raised her hoof to give her attacker a
conk-punch.

"Wait, Bo." McMoo pulled her away.
"I recognize him."

"I recognize his hat," Pat added. "He's a Prime *Moo*-ver from the twenty-sixth century. One of the C.I.A.'s bosses!"

McMoo grinned. "Holstein, isn't it? It was you who took us into the future and asked us to join the C.I.A. all that time ago."

"Indeed it was," said Holstein, dusting himself down.

"Sorry I whumped you," Bo apologized, "but you shouldn't have tried to catch me. I thought you were an F.B.I. agent."

"I thought *you* were one!" Holstein explained. "You see—"

"WHAT'S ALL THE NOISE?" Bessie boomed from the upstairs window. "SOMEONE UP TO MONKEY BUSINESS?"

"*Cow* business, actually." McMoo

bundled Holstein, Pat and Bo into the bushes just as Bessie's flushed red face appeared at the window again, her eyes like bloodshot spotlights searing into every corner of the garden.

"I've got the best view in the house from these windows," she bellowed. "I'll see you, whoever you are – and I'll sock you one!"

As she lumbered off, Pat gave a sigh of relief.

"Beastly woman," Holstein grumbled. "I wish you lived far away from her in the future, where cows exist in freedom and peace."

"If we did, it would change history," McMoo reminded him. "And the C.I.A. is supposed to keep history on track."

"That's why I'm here," Holstein agreed. "It seems the F.B.I. is trying to commit a new time-crime, codenamed Operation Viking. They have broken into several zoos and stolen the animals – everything from an octopus to a pair of lions – and transported them into the past."

Bo frowned. "Why?"

"And what's it got to do with Vikings?" wondered Pat.

"That's what we want you all to find out," said Holstein. "When I saw Bo hovering in the sky like that, I feared she was an F.B.I. agent using a stolen bird to attack you."

"So *that's* why you roped me," Bo realized.

Holstein gave McMoo a sharp look. "If you'd only repaired your time-telephone instead of inventing mechanical wings, Director Yak wouldn't have had to ask me to come here at all!"

"Ooops!" McMoo looked sheepish. "I didn't realize it was on the blink."

"Where is Yakky-babes, anyway?" asked Bo.

"He is busy investigating a prison-break back in our own time," Holstein

informed her. "A highly dangerous F.B.I.
mad scientist is on the loose."

"Yak will soon catch him," said Pat
confidently.

"Let's hope so," said Holstein.
"Meanwhile, having traced recent F.B.I.
time-trails, we believe Operation Viking
is taking place in the year 878 AD."

"878 AD?" McMoo beamed. "That's
when the Vikings were at their height. A
time of looting and pillaging! Alfred the
Great! Big hairy peasants!"

"Shhh!" Pat hushed him. "You'll have
Bessie back at the window again!"

Holstein handed McMoo a small component. "This place-date data chip will direct your Time Shed to the general area. From there, you must hunt down the enemy — and stop whatever they're planning." He huffed quietly. "And I do hope this is the last time I have to give a mission briefing while covered by a bush!"

"Seems quite fitting to me," said McMoo. "We are *undercover* agents, after all!"

Pat gulped. "And now it's time to prove it — in the past."

"So, come on!" Bo burst from the bushes, wings still askew, and struck a heroic pose. "It's time for action, boys — Cows In Action!"

Chapter Two

ENTER . . . THE VIKINGS!

While Holstein crept back to his time
machine in the next field, McMoo hared
off to his shed, with Pat and Bo close
behind. *WHAM!* He slammed open the
doors and turned a big bronze lever.
"Here we go, then!"

At once, the shed began to rattle and
shake. Gleaming computer panels swung
out from behind the wooden walls, and
a horseshoe-shaped bank of controls rose
up from the muddy floor. Cables in the
corners crackled with power, pumping
energy into the mysterious systems that
worked the ramshackle craft. A computer
screen came down from the rafters, and

a costume cupboard crammed with outfits for every place, time and occasion popped up from behind some hay bales. Pat looked around him with a familiar thrill of excitement – the dowdy cowshed had become the incredible *Time Shed*, ready to take them to anywhere – and any*when* – in the world.

"Stick the kettle on, Pat, while I see where we're going." McMoo plugged the place-date data chip into the console. "Aha! The north Dorset coast, 2nd April, 878 AD. Not long before Alfred the Great defeated the Vikings at the Battle of Edington . . ."

"I think I've heard of the Vikings." Bo scowled. "Didn't they used to go round wearing helmets with cow horns stuck onto them?"

"That's a *mooth* – er, myth, I mean." McMoo yanked down on the take-off lever and the Time Shed thrummed and rattled. "No one's ever found a horned

Viking helmet."

"Lucky for the Vikings," said Bo, "or else I'd punch them."

"That might not be wise," McMoo warned her, checking his instruments as the shed rode the waves of time to the distant past. "Computer – let's have the Viking file."

The big screen in the rafters glowed into life.

++ Vikings. ++ Brave, fierce Norse warriors from Scandinavia. ++ Active from around AD 700–1100. ++ Master ship-builders. ++ Great explorers and navigators. ++ Many invaded other countries to steal treasure and conquer the local population. ++

Pat took a nervous sip of tea. "They don't sound very nice, do they?"

McMoo drained his own bucket in a single colossal gulp. "By 878 the Vikings had managed to conquer most of England. Only the kingdom of Wessex held out – thanks to King Alfred."

Bo yawned. "What was so good about this Alfred the Grape?"

"*Great*," Pat and the professor corrected her.

"Sorry," said Bo. "What was so *great* about this Alfred the Grape?"

McMoo sighed. "At the time we'll be arriving, Alfred's been defeated by the Vikings – but he never stops fighting back. Later this year he'll raise an army

16

and turn the tables on the Vikings, forcing them out of his land." McMoo's voice began to rise with enthusiasm. "That paves the way for him to become the first king of the Anglo-Saxons, the English people. He'll make laws fairer, he'll be a champion of reading and writing in English, he'll start up the first English navy and build fortified settlements so his people can protect themselves from future enemy attacks." He looked at Bo. "Is that great enough for you?"

"It's all right, I suppose," said Bo. "But could he dance? Could he groove on down to some phat beats? Huh?" She grinned. "Now, that would be great!"

"You're starting to *grate* on my nerves!" complained Pat.

"Shh, you two," said McMoo as, with the clinking of a hundred invisible milk bottles, the Time Shed slammed back down into existence. "We've arrived!

Let's see where we are." He ran to the door and threw it open . . .

To find a spear flying towards him!

"Whoa!" McMoo ducked as the weapon whistled past his ear and thunked into a hay bale, then quickly slammed the door shut again.

Pat charged over to help the professor up, while Bo opened the door a crack and peered out suspiciously. "If someone wants a fight," she growled, "I'm the cow to give it to them."

"I think it was just a wild throw," said McMoo as he and Pat joined her by the door. "There's no fighting going on – it's a chase . . ."

Pat saw that the shed had landed in a grassy field beside a hedgerow. On the other side of the hedge was a muddy track. An angry mob of rough-looking humans was surging past, waving sticks, spears and stones.

"Down with the Danes!" someone

shouted.

"Drive them out!" bawled another.

"Who are the Danes?" asked Pat.

"It's what the English call the Vikings," McMoo murmured as the surly gang vanished round the corner. "Obviously not *all* Norse raids on England were successful. This lot are being repelled." He pointed towards the sea, which was visible over a clutch of nearby grassy hills. "I'll bet the Vikings are trying to get back to their ship – it's probably close by."

"Holstein said that Vikings were key

to the F.B.I. plan," mused Pat. "Maybe the ones being chased know something about it."

McMoo nodded. "And if they do, we need to know it too."

"Then let's change into human gear and hope we can gain on the Danes!" said Bo.

McMoo was already racing over to the costume cupboard. "You'd better take those wings off first."

"Yeah, yeah," said Bo as McMoo threw a rough mauve dress across to her. "Yuk! Is this what Vikings wore?"

"If we pretend to be Viking raiders, we could be killed on the spot," said McMoo, passing a green tunic and a pair of simple, scratchy breeches to Pat. "Best we fit in with

the Anglo-Saxon locals." He clambered
into a grand blue outfit with a cloak,
then handed slim silver bands to Pat and
Bo. "Here – your ringblenders."

Pat secured the gadget in his snout,
while Bo did the same with hers.
Ringblenders were clever C.I.A. devices
that projected an optical illusion. Any
cow that dressed like a human would
seem to *be* a human, even speaking the
local lingo. Only other cattle – such as
F.B.I. agents – would see through the
disguise at once . . .

"There!" McMoo stuck in his own ringblender and smiled at his friends. "To human eyes we look like well-to-do Anglo-Saxons – and so the Vikings will think we're worth a tasty ransom." He opened the doors and set off after the angry rabble. "Come on – let's see if we can get ourselves captured by a bunch of vicious Vikings!"

"How are we going to get ourselves captured by those Vikings when they're so busy running away?" asked Bo, jogging alongside him with Pat.

McMoo watched the angry peasants pursue the Norsemen along a winding downhill path. "We need to reach the Vikings ahead of that mob." He turned to Pat. "You're good at finding things, Pat. Can you find us a short cut?"

"I'll try." Pat gazed around and sniffed the air. "Hmm . . . let's try that thicket there." He pointed to a tangle of gnarled trees. "If we can get through that lot

22

we should come
out close to the
beach."

"No sooner
mooed than done!"
Bo charged up to the
thicket and, with a flurry
of kung-moo chops
and high-speed hooves,
beat a path through the thick
undergrowth. "There we go!"

Pat led McMoo and Bo at a gallop
out of the little wood and onto a
steep, sandy hillside. Sure-hoofed, he
picked a direct downward path over
the treacherous terrain, heading for
a thin strip of beach. A long, graceful
boat, shallow in depth and narrow in
width, stood on the sand. There was a
single white square sail and six benches
for twelve oarsmen. A carved wooden
dragon's head crowned the front and
rear of the vessel.

McMoo skidded to a stop at the sight of it. "Look at that! A genuine Viking longship. Light enough for the crew to carry, they could steer it through even shallow waters—"

"Better save the lecture till later, Prof!" Bo interrupted as shouts and yells further along the beach announced the arrival of a rabble of distant figures, fast approaching, with an angry mob close behind. "The Vikings are coming – straight for us!"

Chapter Three

THE PILLAGE IDIOTS

"Er, is it my imagination," said Pat, "or do those Vikings look a bit . . . weedy?"

McMoo frowned. "You're right!" The twelve Norsemen were puffing and panting, red in the face behind their beards and long moustaches. They were all shapes and sizes, wearing leather armour under their long woollen shirts, and tatty trousers bound to the knee with crisscrossed straps of fabric.

One of the Vikings was tubbier than the rest. He wore a metal helmet, a scrappy fur cloak and a terrified expression as he took in the three C.I.A. agents loitering beside the longship. He

and his men skidded to a sudden, sandy
stop.

"We're cut off, Gruntbag!" One Viking,
young and lanky, gazed imploringly at
the big cloaked man. "What do we do?"

"I'll think of something, Ivar."
Gruntbag, clearly the Viking in charge,
looked behind him at the angry Anglo-
Saxons approaching and whimpered like
a petrified puppy.

"Hello. We surrender!" called McMoo brightly. "Take us hostage, please."

"Yes, we're worth a fortune," said Pat.

"Especially me," Bo added with a wink.

Gruntbag stared in amazement. Then he beamed. "D'you hear that, lads? We've got ourselves some captives at last!"

"Real proper prisoners!" cheered Ivar.

"It's a miracle!" An old Viking broke into a feeble victory dance.

Pat swapped a baffled look with Bo while McMoo cleared his throat noisily. "Er, do you think you could celebrate once you've got away from that mad mob?"

"Death to the invaders!" roared an angry Anglo-Saxon.

28

"Burn their dragon ship!" screamed another. "And toast their bottoms on the flames!"

"You may have a point, Englishman." Gruntbag waved at his men. "Launch the boat, lads, and let's set sail for safer shores."

Bo sighed impatiently as the Vikings struggled to lift their longship. "Give it here," she grumbled, and helped to heave it into the water with a stupendous splash. "Now, let's start rowing!"

"What a maiden!" Gruntbag gazed
at Bo with admiration as his band
scrambled to their places beside the oars.
"Heave! Heave!"

With Pat, Bo and McMoo lending
their strength to the rowing, the Viking
longship finally began to pull away from
the shore.

But the Anglo-Saxons hurled spears
and flaming torches after them. "Look!"
one bellowed. "The Danes have taken
prisoners!"

"Yes!" Gruntbag yelled back. "Isn't it
splendid?"

The angry shouts grew fainter as
the speedy Viking vessel powered away
across the water. Soon the only sounds
were the grunts and gasps of sweating
Vikings.

"There," said McMoo, lowering his
oar. "That should do."

"Phew!" said Gruntbag, mopping his
forehead with his moustache. "Thanks

for your help, prisoners.
Although I'm
surprised you gave
it."

"*I'm* surprised
that blokes as weedy
as you would attack a
whole village," Bo retorted.

"We didn't attack them," said
Gruntbag indignantly. "We only asked
them if they knew where all the Viking
scouting parties have disappeared to."

"Disappeared?" Pat echoed.

"Our ruler has sent four ships and
many men to scout out this part of the
coast," Ivar explained. "He wants to
know how well defended it is and what
loot might be taken."

"Arlik the Mighty was first to sail two
weeks ago," Gruntbag continued. "But
he hasn't been seen since. Nor have any
of those valorous Vikings who followed.
At least, I don't *think* they have."

Ivar sighed. "Whenever we ask the locals, they always run out and try to kill us."

"You can't really blame them," said McMoo. "You Vikings have ransacked and pillaged an awful lot of England."

"*We* haven't," Ivar protested. "We haven't done any pillaging."

A rat-faced man beside him nodded gloomily. "Or ransacking."

"I once ran *in* a sack," said an incredibly short Viking with a squeaky voice. "Does that count?"

"No, Henmir," said Gruntbag sadly as a shaggy-haired Viking with an eyepatch pulled out a stringed musical instrument. "And before you start, Sven, playing a lute is *not* the same as looting!"

Bo peered down at a chest full of swords and axes. "Haven't you ever

32

used these weapons, then?"

"Are you mad, girl?" Gruntbag looked appalled. "Those things are sharp! We could cut ourselves."

"Anyway, they're too heavy to carry very far," Ivar added.

Lowering her voice, Bo turned to Pat and McMoo. "This must be the most rubbishy bunch of Vikings in the world."

McMoo looked thoughtful. "Their ruler has obviously lost a lot of good men around here – perhaps he sent this lot along to get lost too!"

"I don't suppose we'll learn much here." Pat surveyed the ragbag bunch and couldn't help but feel a bit sorry for them. "Where do you think the proper Vikings went?"

Suddenly the ship lurched as though a whale was trying to rise beneath it. Ivar screamed like a baby and the rat-faced man fainted dead away.

Gruntbag clutched his stomach. "What in Odin's name was that?"

"It's a sea monster!" hissed Ivar.

"There's no such thing," said Pat. "Er, is there, Professor?"

"Let's take a look." While McMoo lay down and pressed his ear to the wooden deck, Bo and Pat peered about on either side of the narrow vessel. There wasn't a cloud in the sky, the water was calm and the nearest land a distant strip of chalky green.

WHUMM! Again, the longship shook under some massive impact.

McMoo jumped up. "There's something huge moving about directly underneath us," he cried, grabbing an oar. "Start rowing, everyone!"

SLAMM!

"Do as he says!" Gruntbag told his ragged crew.

But suddenly a huge, fleshy white tentacle burst from the water at the rear of the ship! Sven stood up and screamed as the fat tendril curled around his waist and jerked him up into the air. "Help! Help!"

Short and squeaky Henmir was grabbed by another groping tentacle, but McMoo caught hold of his ankles and tried to twist him free.

"Help me!" the professor gasped.

Pat and Bo bundled over and grabbed McMoo, just as the giant tentacle flexed, almost pulling him and Henmir overboard. McMoo gasped as he noticed a huge yellow eye glaring up at him from the grey-green sea.

The eye sat in a bloated body patterned black and white – like a cow! – and two colossal pointed horns curved out from either side of its bulk.

"It's some kind of giant octopus!" Pat shouted.

Bo frowned. "Looks more like an *ox*-topus to me."

McMoo clung grimly onto Henmir's short little legs. "Whatever it is," he panted, "I think we've found out what happened to all those missing Vikings."

"The sea monster has drowned them all," groaned Gruntbag as more massive tentacles snaked over the sides of the longship. "And now it will do the same to us!"

Chapter Four

TROUBLE FOR SHORE

Still straining to hold onto Henmir,
McMoo, Pat and Bo stared down at
the sinister sea-cow creature as it
brought the struggling Sven towards its
gaping gob.

"It's going to eat him!" Henmir
squeaked.

But then the oxtopus blew a big
yellow bubble around the Viking – and
tugged him under the water. Sven was
lost from sight . . .

When the monster's tentacle resurfaced
a few seconds later, it was Viking-free.

"Don't let me go," Henmir begged.
"Or that'll happen to me!"

"I've had enough of this eight-legged bully," gasped Bo. "Or rather, I've *udder-nuff!*" Jumping up, she fired a long, supersonic squirt of milk right into the eye of the oxtopus. The water churned and frothed as the beast gave a nerve-shredding cry and sank beneath the surface, tugging its twitching tentacles after it.

Gruntbag flopped onto the deck, panting. "Thank Odin, it's gone."

"But it could be back soon." McMoo plonked the white-faced Henmir on his rowing bench. "So we must all start rowing. We need to get out of here."

Ivar picked up his oar sadly. "Poor Sven."

Pat shook his head as he grabbed an oar too. "That sea-monster blew a bubble around him before it dragged him under . . . I wonder why?"

"Perhaps it was chewing gum," suggested Bo, biceps bulging as she started to row.

"I think we need to investigate that creature a little more closely," said McMoo. "But without putting Gruntbag and his crew at risk."

"Unhoist the sail, lads," called Gruntbag, "and we'll head for Wessex's shores."

Pat frowned. "But you'll be attacked by the locals again!"

"Wessex is under Viking rule," Gruntbag reminded him. "But when our ruler learns we have come back with no news of his *real* warriors, he'll probably slay us himself!"

The Vikings beached their longship on a quiet stretch of coast and fell gratefully down on the wet sand, panting for breath. Gruntbag produced a long cow horn from a pouch at his side, drank water from it, then offered it to McMoo.

"Call that a cup?" Bo scowled at the Viking. "How'd you like it if we slurped milk out of your ear?"

"Shh," hissed McMoo, with a quick smile at the baffled Dane. "A lot of early humans used drinking horns. We're undercover, remember?"

Pat sighed. "At least it's a nice day. Hardly a cloud in the sky."

Bo pointed to an oval cloud out at sea, white with darker patches that promised rain. "*That* cloud's been around for ages. I noticed it before we were grabbed by that crummy oxtopus."

"It can't be the same cloud," McMoo told her. "The wind's been helping to push us along – it would push clouds along too."

Bo shrugged. "Well, it hasn't. Those grey spots are in just the same place – I noticed 'cos it reminded me of a cow."

"Anyway, a bit of rain's the last thing we have to worry about." McMoo took another slurp from the drinking horn and jumped up. "Well, Gruntbag, being your helpless prisoners has been a wonderful experience, but now we'd best be off."

"Oh!" The colour drained from Gruntbag's face and he gulped loudly. "Well, it was nice knowing you all."

"Aren't you going to even *try* and stop us?" Bo asked him incredulously.

Gruntbag shook his head, pointing past her to the top of the cliffs. "Not when English soldiers are about to attack!"

Pat turned and craned his neck to find a grim-looking gang of twelve men with bows and arrows and spears lining the cliff top.

"Ho, Danes!" called a gaunt, red-haired fellow. "Move and you die!"

Henmir fell over in a dead faint.

"That didn't count!" squeaked Ivar quickly. Bo looked at Gruntbag. "I thought you said Vikings were in charge of Wessex?"

"There are small bands of Englishmen who resist our rule," Gruntbag admitted. "Just our luck to find one."

The newcomers scrambled down a narrow path in the cliff face, led by the red-haired man. "We'd heard tell of Danish ships in these waters and came looking," he said. "It seems our thirst for battle will be quickly quenched . . ."

"We've had it!" sobbed Ivar, and Gruntbag hung his head.

"Play along," McMoo hissed, then beamed up at the Englishmen. "Evening all! You can put away your weapons. My friends and I have just captured these Viking raiders for you."

"You have?" The red-haired man

paused mid-stride and gave McMoo a penetrating stare. "A nobleman, a boy and a pretty maiden have subdued a Danish raiding party with no arms?"

"No arms?" Bo waved with both her hooves. "What do you think these are, dummy?"

A bald, burly guard raised his spear. "How dare you address your king in such a fashion, girl!"

"Hold, Bryce," the red-haired man said smoothly. "I like a maid with fire in her belly."

Bo winked. "And milk in her udder?"

"*Moo*-ving on . . ." McMoo jumped in quickly. "King, eh? Don't tell me – you're Alfred the Great!"

"I am Alfred, son of Ethelwulf, King of Wessex," the red-haired man informed him.

"That *is* great!" McMoo beamed.

"You have done well to capture these Danes," said Alfred. "There may be much they can tell us about the wicked plans of their countrymen."

As Gruntbag and his friends gave a sigh of relief, McMoo bowed down low, motioning Pat and Bo to do the same. "Gracious sire, I am Angus, and these are my wards, Patrick and, er . . .

Boadicea. We are travellers, and came across these Danes upon the shore."

Pat nodded. "Their boat ran into trouble with a sea-creature."

"I have heard lately that a great terror rises from the deep to threaten only the Danes," said Alfred with satisfaction. "No

46

ships of *ours* have been affected."

"So it's a picky sea-creature," said McMoo thoughtfully. "Very interesting."

"Excuse me, King Alfred," said Pat politely. "I don't mean to be rude, but you don't look very king-like at the moment."

"I am in disguise," Alfred replied loftily. "Since the Danes overran my castle and my kingdom three months ago, I have been forced to live out in the marshes with a small band of heroic men."

"Your private life's your own business, Al," Bo told him.

Alfred glared at Gruntbag and the Vikings. "We have launched many surprise attacks on our invaders," he went on. "Why, once I even disguised myself as a travelling minstrel and walked right into the Danes' camp, so I could overhear their private plans." He chuckled. "That's how I knew to expect Viking forces in these waters."

"And have you burned the cakes

too?" asked McMoo eagerly. "Or hasn't that happened yet?"

"Eh?" said Alfred.

McMoo nodded. "There's a story that says you hid out undercover in a peasant woman's house and she asked you to mind her cakes while they cooked in her oven, but you got distracted and the cakes burned and she clobbered you 'cos she didn't know who you were—" He clamped a hoof over his own mouth. "Whoops, sorry! I'm getting carried away. That must happen in your future. Forget I said anything."

Alfred looked at him blankly. "I have no idea what you're talking about."

"You'll understand this," Bo said grimly. "Look over there – loads more Vikings heading straight for us, in a big boat!"

"What?" Alfred and his men turned to follow her gaze – and gasped in dismay.

A huge longship was cutting through the waves towards the shore.

"Oh, no!" Gruntbag looked horrified. "I recognize that sail . . . That's Arlik's ship."

McMoo frowned. "Arlik the Mighty, who hasn't been seen since he disappeared a fortnight ago?"

"Arlik the drowned!" Ivar wailed. "That's a ghost ship!"

Pat felt his spine tingle as the mysterious craft sailed closer. "Then we'd better get ready to be haunted!"

Chapter Five

ATTACK OF THE ZOMBIE VIKINGS

"Ghosts? Rubbish!" cried Alfred. "That ship looks solid enough to me – and so does its crew!"

"Something's different about them," Bo declared. "Professor, you said Vikings didn't wear horns on their helmets – but this lot do!"

As the longship sped closer, Pat saw she was right. "They've all got horns on their helmets. And that one at the front has got the biggest of all. Even his face is gleaming like it's metal—" He broke off in shock. "Oh, no. Tell me I'm seeing things."

"If you are, it's catching," muttered Bo.

McMoo nodded gravely. "The crew might be human, but their captain is a *ter-moo-nator!*"

Pat's blood chilled at the thought of the F.B.I.'s toughest field-agents. Part bull, part robot, ter-moo-nators had no emotions – or e-*moo*-tions for that matter – and were ruthless in the execution of their diabolical duties.

What was this one doing with a gang of drowned Vikings and their sunken boat?

The ter-moo-nator was certainly dressed for the part, Pat reflected – with chain mail, iron bands on his arms and an impressive yellow beard. The ringblender he wore would fool all humans into thinking he was a regular Viking, rather than a cyber-bull in fancy dress.

"Where did they come from?" murmured McMoo. "And what do they want?"

Oblivious to McMoo's interest, Alfred turned to his band of men. "I have a plan, lads. We'll take the Viking dress of our captives here, and trick these newcomers into thinking we're their countrymen. Then we'll attack and seize their ship!"

"Spare us our pants, sir!" begged Gruntbag.

Alfred turned up his nose. "For the sake of decency, you can wear our clothes."

"'Tis a fine plan, sire!" A long-haired archer grinned. "With Arlik's vessel and this smaller one, we'll be able to make bolder attacks than ever!"

"I beseech your majesty to be careful," said McMoo. "These are no ordinary Vikings."

"Neither are these." Bryce lifted up the stumpy Henmir. "This one's uniform wouldn't fit a plump hamster!"

Alfred pointed to a cave in the cliff face. "Men, take the Danes inside so we can swap clothes." He smiled at McMoo. "You must hide there with your fellow travellers until the battle is done."

"Wait!" called Gruntbag as Bryce tried to pull him into the cave. "Look, rowing there by the mast – it's Arlik himself!"

"And beside him is Karl the Crusher, who led the next expedition," said Ivar in wonder. "And beside *him* is Halfdan the Hole-puncher . . . Ooh, and Sam the Scar-maker."

"The very men we were sent to find!" Gruntbag agreed.

"I'm not so sure they're just men any longer . . ." McMoo stared, transfixed, at the crew's strangely leathery faces, marked with black and white – almost like cowhide. They rowed in synchronized silence, more like robots than men.

"Look!" Pat pointed to a far

scrawnier-looking Viking. "There's Sven!"

"Back from his watery grave!" squeaked Henmir. "And wearing finer armour than he ever did in life."

"Silence, Danes!" Alfred snapped as Gruntbag and his gang were dragged inside the cave. "Take no joy in seeing your friends, for soon they will be vanquished."

McMoo, Pat and Bo kept a tense lookout as the longship crossed the last few hundred metres to shore. The ter-moo-nator and his gang remained impassive, standing still as sculptures, apparently oblivious to all . . .

"Where would Sven find a natty new outfit under the sea?" McMoo wondered.

Suddenly a cracking *BOOM* shuddered out from the sky like a supersonic thunderclap. Bo looked out to sea and gasped. "That cloud I saw before – the one that never moved . . . It's moving now!"

McMoo peered through his specs in disbelief as the black and white oval cloud blew towards them at incredible speed. "It's like nothing I've ever seen before!"

Just then, Alfred strode out of the cave with his men close behind, all done up in Danish clothes. "How do we look?" he asked grandly as, with another thunderclap, the curious cloud halted overhead and burst into torrential rain, like a fluffy sponge wrung out by a giant. The drops were heavy and hot, falling hard enough to sting Pat's skin.

"This isn't rainwater, it tastes like chemicals!" McMoo coughed and spluttered. "Shelter, everyone!" He pushed

Pat and Bo into the mouth of the cave.

But as the prow of Arlik's ship scraped up onto the shore, the dismal downpour stopped and the impossible cloud sped away inland, vanishing over the cliff tops as if steered by some invisible force.

"Who cares about a little foul-tasting rain?" hissed Alfred, gripping his sword. "Be ready to fight when I give the signal, men. We'll wait till they jump down from their ship . . ."

But the ter-moo-nator and his legion of horn-headed Vikings stayed put. "I am Mookow the Terrible," the F.B.I. agent proclaimed in a loud, grating voice. "Since you escaped our sea-creature, we have come to collect you ourselves."

57

Alfred looked blankly at Bryce. "What do these Vikings speak of?"

"You are mistaken," grated Mookow. "We are not Vikings. We are *bull*-kings."

"Bull-kings?" Pat echoed.

"Shhh," said McMoo, and Pat had rarely seen him look so worried. "We can't afford to miss any of this."

The ter-moo-nator glared at Alfred. "You and your men will come with us. You must become bull-kings too."

"Attack!" cried Alfred. He raised his sword high over his head . . .

And it began to melt like an ice cream in the sun!

"Your weapon, sire!" Bryce cried.

Alfred pointed to his archer's arrow-tips, which were dribbling like hot wax. "And *your* weapons too!"

"*All* their weapons!" McMoo realized.

With horror, Pat saw that it was true. Alfred's guards groaned and gasped as their swords splattered into molten puddles and their shields fell apart. Chain mail sagged and stretched as though made from melted cheese, then flopped around their ankles like moth-chewed knickers. The metal in their helmets ran like snail-trails down their cheeks and foreheads.

While his fellow Danes cowered out of sight, Gruntbag had crept forward cautiously to join McMoo in the mouth of the cave. "What witchcraft is this?" he whispered.

"It's the rain!" said McMoo. "Something in it has dissolved all the metal!"

Pat tapped his ringblender. "This is still OK."

"That's from the twenty-sixth century," McMoo reminded him quietly. "That so-called rainwater must contain a substance that destroys older, cruder metals."

"We are defenceless!" shouted Bryce. "My spear is nothing but a stick."

"And my arrows are nothing but twigs," cried the archer.

Only now did Mookow jump down from the ship. "Get them!" he roared.

Suddenly the Vikings – or *bull*-kings – jerked into life! All thirty of them joined the ter-moo-nator on the beach, marching like zombies, their own swords raised and shining in the sunlight – solid, sharp and deadly.

"I can't watch," groaned Gruntbag, retreating to join his quivering men.

"Alfred, run for it!" McMoo shouted.

Mookow himself lunged for Alfred, but the king dived aside just in time. Arlik the Mighty smashed the archer to the ground with a blow from his shield. Karl the Crusher swiped his sword straight through Bryce's spear-shaft. As the other bull-kings joined the attack, Sven tried to join in and raise his sword – but it was too heavy, and he fell over.

"We've got to help Alfred and his people," Pat cried.

"Bo," said McMoo, "are you still

wearing those
mechanical
wings I told you
to put away?"

Bo grinned. "Of
course I am. A girl never
knows when she might have
to take off in a hurry!"

"Good," replied McMoo. "A flying
cow might distract the bull-kings long
enough to tip the fight in our favour."

"Cool!" Bo bent over sharply, ripping
the back of her dress to reveal the
feathered wings. Then she plucked out
her ringblender and ran outside, fiddling
with the controls at her chest. A few
moments later she took to the air with
an excited whoop . . .

And into the fray she flew!

CLANG! CLUNK! She brought both
hooves down on Sven's horned helmet
and kicked the sword from Mookow's
grip. Arlik tried to spike her on his spear

62

but she turned a speedy somersault and tail-whipped him round the chops.

Alfred stared in astonishment. "A cow with angel's wings? Has that rain melted my senses as well as my sword?"

"Let's help her, Pat." McMoo grinned wildly. "I think it's time we showed those Viking zombies how to *really* use a pair of horns!"

Leaving Gruntbag and the others safely hidden in the cave, the C.I.A. agents dashed onto the beach to join the attack at ground level. McMoo's mighty charge brought down three burly bull-kings in one go! Pat quickly belly-slapped their fallen foes before they could rise again.

"Well fought, my friends!" Alfred panted. He broke the remains of a spear over Mookow's head, but the ter-moo-nator socked him with a steel hoof and knocked him out cold.

"You big beefy bully!" Bo quickly shot a superfast, extra-creamy jet of milk into Mookow's face. Spluttering with rage, the ter-moo-nator leaped into the air with a speed that belied his bionic bulk. He grabbed Bo's ankle and yanked her savagely down to earth –

THUD!

Bo's mechanical wings crunched beneath her as she hit the sand and crumpled in a silent heap . . .

Chapter Six

VIKING DISLIKING

"Little Bo!" Pat shouted in horror.

"We've got to help her." McMoo started up the shore towards Bo. But then Sven marched into their path, dragging his sword behind him. The horns on his helmet were only small and his skin was not yet patterned like the other bull-kings – but he shared their blank stare.

"Let us pass, Sven," said McMoo. "We helped you before – don't you recognize us?"

But as Sven struggled harder to raise his sword, Sam the Scar-maker pushed him aside and started swinging an axe at Pat and McMoo, driving the agents

back towards the sea. And with Bo and Alfred both brought down, Pat realized that the English forces were faring badly. Bryce and another soldier struggled up – only for Halfdan the Hole-puncher to knock them down again. The archer tried to run to his king's side, only to be conked unconscious by Arlik's flying shield ... Man after man was falling to the power of Mookow and his belligerent bull-kings.

Now, Mookow himself and two other bull-kings joined Sam in attacking the unarmed Pat and McMoo. "Ringblenders detected," the ter-moo-nator hissed, swiping viciously with his axe. "C.I.A. agents must be destroyed!"

With an obedient nod, Sam and the bull-kings fought even more fiercely.

"No way past them," McMoo muttered, "so we'll have to retreat. Come on, Pat, into the water!"

Pat followed the professor, swimming out to sea. As he looked past the ter-moo-nator, he saw Alfred stirring weakly on the shore. "Get away, sire!" he yelled. Then he felt McMoo's hoof on his, dragging him out deeper into the water until it closed over their heads.

Pat held his breath, waiting in the cold darkness. His head began to spin. His lungs felt ready to pop! But then McMoo pressed something to his lips – Gruntbag's drinking horn! The professor had snapped off the pointed tip so it could be used as a kind of snorkel.

Gratefully Pat pushed one end of the horn above the surface of the water and sucked down a breath of salty air. Then he passed the horn back to McMoo, who did the same. Pat supposed they would have to stay here until Mookow was satisfied they were dead — or at least until he got bored. He only hoped Bo would recover in time to get away as well . . .

Pat wasn't sure how much time passed as he and McMoo struggled to stay submerged in the gloomy water, breathing through the broken horn. But finally McMoo nudged him, and together they broke the surface like a pair of cow-shaped periscopes and waded to shore, using Gruntbag's boat for cover.

"That was close," Pat gasped.

McMoo nodded, wiping his glasses on his wet cloak. "I thought they'd never leave."

"But they have," Pat realized. "And they're carrying passengers!"

Mookow's longship was just departing, and looked to be piled high with the bodies of Alfred's men. Bo was lashed to the carving of a dragon on the boat's prow, struggling furiously. *At least she's alive*, thought Pat grimly.

"Look!" McMoo pointed to the top of the cliffs. Pat glanced up in time to see King Alfred disappear from sight, pursued by four huge bull-kings.

"It looks like Alfred got away," said Pat.

"You'd better get up there and try to keep him safe. Alfred the Great is too important to history to let anything happen to him." McMoo thought hard. "I'll come looking for you when I can – hopefully with Bo."

Pat grinned. "You're going after her?"

"Course I am! I'll take Gruntbag's boat and see if I can find out what Operation Viking is all about," McMoo told him. "Now, off you go!"

"OK," sighed Pat, watching Mookow's longship as it began to dwindle from sight. "Good luck – and keep safe."

McMoo watched proudly as Pat tore away up the steep cliffs – if not like a mountain goat, then very much like a mountain cow. "Right," he breathed, "time I was going . . ." But as he moved round the boat, he noticed a prone figure lying half buried in the sand.

"Sven!" cried Gruntbag, peeping out

from the nearby cave-mouth. "Is he dead?"

McMoo stooped to examine the fallen bull-king. "No. Mookow must've decided he was too weak and puny compared to the other bull-kings. Let's take this silly horned helmet off . . ." He tugged. And tugged. And tugged again.

Ivar came out of hiding, one eyebrow raised. "I thought *we* were the feeble ones. Is it stuck?"

"No, it's not just stuck." McMoo frowned. "Those horns are a *part* of him. They stick out through his helmet – but they're growing out of his head!"

Ivar fainted – revealing Henmir hiding behind him. "Growing out of his head?" squeaked the little Viking. "That's crazy!"

"Look at his skin too," said McMoo. "Tanned and shiny, almost like leather . . ."

Gruntbag gulped. "What does it mean?"

"It means 'bull-king' isn't just a fancy name." McMoo looked at him grimly. "Remember that sea-monster? Part ox, part octopus, a whole new form of life? Well, I reckon Sven and the other lost Vikings have been turned into a new form of life too. Bull-kings are half human . . . and half cow!"

Sides aching and panting for breath, Pat managed to catch up with King Alfred near the edge of the wind-blown cliffs. Some horses had been tethered to a tree, and Alfred was readying a white stallion for mounting.

"King Alfred!" the young bullock called. "Wait for me!"

"Boy!" The harried king looked pleased to see him. "Then you got away? I thought you had joined my poor men, captives of that evil Mookow and his sorcerer's cloud. I curse myself for sleeping when I should've been fighting."

"It's not your fault you were knocked out," said Pat. "The prof – I mean, Angus – is planning to follow Mookow, to find his base. If you can raise an army and find some weapons that won't melt in that weird rain, perhaps we can rescue your men. And my sister too."

"I have a base in the marshes of Athelney, to the south," Alfred revealed, pointing a finger. But as Pat gazed over in that direction, he saw something unpleasantly familiar in the sky.

The impossible oval cloud was hovering in the distance, and seemed to be shedding more of its sinister rain!

"Don't tell me *that's* where your base is?" said Pat.

Alfred turned to Pat and nodded grimly. "It would seem this enchanted thundercloud has a grudge against me."

Just then, the four bull-kings scrambled up over the top of the cliff and drew their swords. "Uh-oh," said Pat. "*They've* got a grudge against you too!"

"Quick, boy, get on a horse," cried Alfred. "We must ride to safety!"

Pat chose the strongest-looking horse and clambered on board. It looked back at him with a "You've got to be kidding me" expression, but did its best to hold his weight. And as it staggered away after Alfred's steed, pursued by the remorseless bull-kings, Pat could only hope that safety might be found somewhere in this terrifying time . . .

With a loud grunt and an enormous shove, Professor McMoo launched Gruntbag's longship into the water. "Right!" he cried cheerily to Gruntbag and his crew, lined up on the shore. "Who's coming with me to brave that octopus monster, rescue Bo, and take on Mookow and his heavily armed bull-kings in some mysterious undersea lair that is bound to be chock-full of deadly traps?"

The Vikings looked at each other in shifty silence.

McMoo gave an encouraging smile. "Don't all volunteer at once!"

"I'll come," said Gruntbag reluctantly. "It's my boat, after all – and when our leaders hear how I've messed up this mission, I'll be dead anyway!"

Ivar shook his head. "But if Arlik the Mighty and all the rest couldn't stop Mookow, how can you?"

"Perhaps by using a little brainpower," McMoo suggested.

"I've got a little brain," Henmir piped up. "Is that any good?"

Gruntbag smiled. "I'm glad to have you aboard, my friend."

"Me too." McMoo reached into the boat and heaved out the chest, which had protected the weapons inside from the metal-eating rain. "Ivar, you'd better take these into the cave in case you need to defend yourselves. Hide out there until we get back."

"Thanks," replied Ivar. "What if you *don't* get back?"

"You can pass the time congratulating each other on how right you were to stay behind." McMoo hoisted the sail, which billowed in the breeze. "Now, Mookow's got a head start and a lot more rowers, but we have to keep him in sight. Let's go!"

"Oi! Get me down from here!" Bo huffed and grumbled, struggling against the ropes that lashed her to the front of Mookow's longship. "Where are you taking me?"

"You are an escaped *moo*-tant," the ter-moo-nator informed her. "You must be corrected by Doctor Gaur."

"I'm no moo-tant!" Bo yelled. "And you're the one who'll be corrected

when I get free of these ropes!" Then
she realized the creaking of oars had
stopped. A moment later, the waters
ahead began to seethe and churn, and
the humungous oxtopus rose up from the
deep, its black and white body aquiver,
its thick tentacles stretching out around
the ship. At the sight of Bo, its single
bloodshot eye narrowed.

"Er . . . wotcher." Bo gave the oxtopus
her most appealing smile. "Nice to see
you again. No hard feelings, eh?"

The oxtopus hissed and a yellow
bubble blew
slowly from its
mouth, swelling
to engulf
her . . .

Chapter Seven

THE DEADLY DR GAUR

"Mookow's longship has stopped!" In the little boat, McMoo motioned to Gruntbag and Henmir to put down their oars.

"They must be ready to meet the oxtopus." McMoo pointed to where the black and white beast bobbed in the foaming waters. He watched, alarmed but fascinated, as Bo was engulfed in an enormous glistening bubble blown from the mouth of the oxtopus. Seconds later, the creature caught Alfred's men in more of the sinister-looking bubbles. Then it dragged its prisoners underwater.

"It'll drown them all," Gruntbag gasped.

"I don't think so." McMoo watched as Mookow steered the ship away with his remaining bull-kings, heading eastward

around the Wessex coast. "Those bubbles must hold in the air like some sort of underwater taxi, with the oxtopus as the driver. It probably takes its prisoners to someone hiding down there. And

there's only one way to find out who
that someone is." He took a deep breath.
"We've got to go underwater."

"You mean, let ourselves get attacked
by that – that horrible thing?" Henmir
stammered.

"I hope that's what he means,"
muttered Gruntbag. "Because here it
comes now!"

McMoo's eyes widened. With its first
lot of victims now submerged, the many-
tentacled monster seemed set on finding
fresh targets. It pushed itself through the
water towards them,
and the little longship
rocked so hard it
nearly threw its crew
overboard.

McMoo gasped as
a tentacle wrapped
around his waist and
lifted him high into
the air. He had to hold

onto his spectacles to stop them falling into the sea. "Don't struggle!" McMoo shouted as Henmir and Gruntbag were also grabbed by the gruesome creature. "Remember it just wants to take us down below."

Then he could say no more as a big yellow bubble blew out of the oxtopus's massive mouth and sucked him inside. The thick yellow bubble-skin contained him and the monster's tentacle withdrew. He found himself being forced downward through the deep blue gloom, propelled by the tip of a tentacle towards an enormous white dome on the seabed, big enough to hold hundreds of bulls.

"That must be the F.B.I. base," he murmured, "hidden away from prying eyes."

Gruntbag and Henmir were both bobbing down beside him in their own bubbles. Then McMoo spotted three bizarre creatures emerging from a doorway in the dome. They looked like giant turtles, but their shells were patterned black and white with cow markings, like the oxtopus. Little horns grew on either side of their wrinkled heads. Warily McMoo watched as the cow-turtles swam up to the taxi-bubbles and pushed their three prisoners towards the entrance.

Inside the dome, bright lights shone to reveal a holding area. It was like a car park for longships! Four of the vessels were contained within enormous bubbles to keep them dry. The turtles pushed McMoo, Gruntbag and Henmir further inside, then closed the door. Moments later, large plug holes opened up in the floor and the seawater drained away. Finally, with a plethora of pops, all the bubbles burst, leaving only drops of yellow goo that were washed away with the last of the water.

"Fascinating!" cried McMoo. "This is a kind of airlock. It must fill up with water too so Mookow, the bull-kings and their boats can float back up to the surface in fresh bubbles."

But Gruntbag and Henmir didn't seem to hear him. They were too busy clutching each other tightly. "What place of evil enchantment is this?" Gruntbag whispered. "These walls are not made with wood or stone. And what are these lights that burn bright as suns?"

"I'd love to explain plastic and electricity to you, old fella," McMoo began, "but I think a lecture on homes of the future will have to wait." He pointed to a square panel in the wall that was sliding open. "We've got company."

Two huge, muscular animals prowled into the room, shaking their shaggy manes and baring flesh-tearing teeth. Like the oxtopus and the turtles before them, they were coloured black and white, with curved horns rising up from either side of their heads.

"Lions!" Henmir squeaked. "Lions that look like cows!"

"What's with the cow thing?" wailed Gruntbag.

"Black splodges are very stylish, but I think they look better on cattle." McMoo flinched as the lions roared again. "Though their jaws would look better *off* cattle!"

Suddenly a strange skunk-like creature scuttled out from between the lions. Its black and white markings had morphed into those of a cow too. But unlike the lions, a haze of gas was squirting from its bottom!

"Hold your breath!" McMoo shouted. But it was too late. Henmir and Gruntbag were already sinking to their knees, clutching at their throats, and McMoo's head was beginning to spin

like a top. As he fell to the floor, he heard
the huge growling cow-lions pad closer
...*closer*...

* * *

"Professor . . . Professor, wake up!"

McMoo stirred groggily in his sleep. Wasn't that Little Bo? But she had been captured by the F.B.I., which had to mean . . .

"Yes, wake up, sleepy-head!" came a deep rasping voice. "I wish to question you."

"That's a coincidence. I want to question you too." McMoo opened his eyes and found he was strapped to a stretcher in a cavernous white room that was part hi-tech laboratory, part operating theatre. Bright lights in the ceiling glared down, making trays of surgical tools gleam and glint. Bo, wrapped up in a blanket, was strapped to another stretcher close by. McMoo beamed as he saw her. "Bo, are you all right?"

"Not very," she retorted. "I've been scrunched into sand, tied to a boat, attacked by a bubble-blowing mutant octopus, gassed by a mutant skunk,

dragged through a
maze of corridors by a
mutant lion and almost
bored to death by this
F.B.I. chump!"

McMoo's smile quickly
faded as he took in the burly
brown bull that stood beside her. "Who
are you?"

"I am Taurus Gaur," the bull
announced.

"He's the loony scientist Holstein told
us was on the loose in the twenty-sixth
century," Bo put in. "No wonder poor
Yakky-babes couldn't find him. Gaur's
been here all along!"

"And keeping very busy," Gaur agreed.
Thick metal spectacles sat on top of his
snout, magnifying his brown eyes. He was
wearing a filthy lab coat and his hooves
were stained yellow and green. "You are
my helpless prisoner, Professor. You were a
fool to enter my undersea domain!"

McMoo nodded ruefully. "I've never been able to resist a good undersea domain."

"And yet you are *not* a fool," Gaur went on, "because it was *you* who invented the flying machine this cow was wearing when she was captured, wasn't it?" He held up the bent and battered set of mechanical wings. "I'm afraid these are useless to you now – they were damaged in the struggle and can no longer support your weight." He threw the wings to the floor. "I have heard of you, McMoo."

"And I think I've heard quite enough of you!" The professor blew out a big breath. "Where are Gruntbag and Henmir?"

"Those puny half-pint Vikings, you mean?" Gaur scoffed. "They are not fit to be turned into bull-kings like the

90

other men Mookow dropped off here. I've left them with the cow-lions."

McMoo yawned. "I suppose you're going to threaten to hurt them unless I do as you say?"

"Have a care, Professor." Gaur eyed him stonily. "You might be a genius in your own time, but *I* am the architect of all cowkind's destiny!"

"See?" Bo rolled her eyes at McMoo. "Ever since I woke up here he's been spouting rubbish like that."

Gaur put his hooves on his hips. "It is *not* rubbish. The work I am doing here will change the place of cows in the world for ever." He gave a high-pitched titter. "Eventually it will change every animal on Earth. Even the human animal."

"Into cows?" McMoo's eyes narrowed. "The octopus, the lions, the turtles, the skunk . . . I assume the F.B.I. stole them from the zoos in the twenty-sixth century. But what have you done to them?"

"I've made them into moo-tants!" Again, Gaur chuckled. "It's easy when you know the secret of moo-goo!"

"*Who*-goo?" Bo echoed blankly.

Gaur grabbed a test tube from the table behind him and waggled it in the C.I.A. agents' faces. "Moo-goo! The chemical wonder substance I invented. Any animal who eats the stuff takes on the characteristics of a cow – or a bull, of course – and becomes my mindless servant."

"So that's how you trained the oxtopus and all those other poor animals to bring us here," McMoo realized. "And why those kidnapped Vikings are working for you."

"But why bother making them look like cows?" asked Bo.

"Because cows are BEST, silly!"

Gaur cackled with delight and pressed a button on a control panel. A section of white wall slid upwards to reveal a glass inspection panel, allowing them to look into a room beyond, covered with vegetation.

McMoo felt a shiver from his nose to his tail at the sight of a horned pony, black and white like a cow, grazing on long grass beside a weird ape-creature

with hooves. "What have you done?"

"As well as the moo-tants you've already met, I've turned horses into cow-horses, a monkey into a *moo*nkey, and . . ."

Gaur sniggered as an ostrich-type bird waddled into sight, displaying its bright pink udder. "Yes – I have even made an emu into an e-*moo*. And that's just for starters . . ."

"I suppose Mookow thought Bo was an escaped specimen," said the professor coldly.

Gaur tutted. "Mookow is a mechanical mutton-head for thinking that *anything* can escape from my stronghold."

Bo smiled sweetly. "Just give us time."

"But time is exactly what you do not have," Gaur gloated. "Now you have both blundered into my clutches, I intend to gain the professor's help with a teeny tiny problem I have. You and the two half-pints will die if he refuses."

"I knew it," said McMoo. "Go on, then. What's your beef? If you'll pardon the expression."

"The Vikings are slow to react to moo-goo. I can control human minds, but they are able to resist the full effect of the biological changes." Gaur shook his head. "This simply will not do. I want them to grow bigger horns, and hooves as well. I want their cow-colours to be brighter. I want them to grow huge udders that blast milk in all directions . . ."

"You're crazy!" cried McMoo. "Why do you want to change humans and animals at all?"

Gaur loomed over him. "At this point in history, the Vikings are at the height of their powers, the fiercest and most feared raiders and invaders anywhere in the world. All other humans fear them and respect them."

"Except for King Alfred," Bo reminded him.

"Precisely. In a matter of months, Alfred will defeat a massive Viking army at the Battle of Edington. The Danes' reputation will be badly damaged." An even loopier gleam had stolen into Gaur's crossed eyes. "But if Alfred is turned into a bull-king he will fight *for* us instead of against us. He will help us capture the rulers of other countries . . ."

"Helped by your handy cloud of metal-eating rain," McMoo concluded. "That dreadful drizzle will destroy the Anglo-Saxons' weapons so they can't fight back, and disintegrate their tools so they can't fend for themselves."

"Quite." Gaur snorted. "The metal-mush cloud is Mookow's contribution to this operation. It can be steered anywhere by remote control – that's quite clever, I suppose . . ."

"Clever? It's hideous!" McMoo snapped. "Without metal, humans won't be able to develop their technology. History will be completely changed."

"But metal from the future is not affected, as you have seen," said Gaur. "Once humans realize that bull-kings alone wield metal weapons, that their former rulers now fight in the name of cattle, humans will come to fear and respect cows too. They will stop farming our kind."

McMoo winced. "Meanwhile, you're busy giving every animal a moo-goo makeover. It will seem as though cows have taken over the planet."

"And so they will!" Gaur rubbed

his stained hooves together with evil anticipation. "My moo-tants will replace all normal animals while the bull-kings conquer the world of humans. Then my F.B.I. masters will join me from the future and rule over everything – masters of an Earth where all life reflects their image. Human history will end in 878 AD – and the cow reign of terror will begin!"

"Professor, he's bonkers!" Bo groaned. "What are we going to do?"

"You will obey me, of course." Gaur pointed to a red cable snaking out from both stretchers to a kind of plug socket in the wall. "I have wired these trolleys to the power supply and can electrify them at any time I choose."

McMoo sighed. "Aren't you taking this mad scientist stuff a bit far?"

"Very funny, Professor." Gaur guffawed and snorted. "But if you choose to defy me, you shall be barbecued where you lie!"

Chapter Eight

THE VALLEY OF FEAR

"Whoa!" Pat slowed his horse in a quiet grassy valley hemmed in by forest. He and Alfred had been riding at full gallop for what seemed like hours. Pat's horse was gasping for breath; if he didn't give it a rest it would surely collapse.

"Why have you stopped?" Alfred reined in his own horse and circled Pat impatiently. "We must find out if my stockade at Athelney is safe."

100

"That cloud has been raining over Athelney, remember?" said Pat. "Your weapons might have melted away by now."

Just then, a rustling and clattering from the trees nearby made Alfred hold his hand up for silence. Pat looked around for a hiding place, but it was too late. A ragged band of men charged out from the forest, clutching broken sticks and clearly terrified. When they saw Alfred, their eyes lit up and they fell to their knees before him.

"Sire!" panted one. "You must flee, there is danger! Strange Vikings on stranger steeds are fast approaching."

"They must be trying to catch us in a pincer movement," Pat realized.

"Did you come from Athelney?" Alfred demanded of his subjects. "The sticks you carry, were they once spears?"

"Truly you are the wisest of kings," said one of the men, impressed. "A terrible rain fell – it stole our blades and spearheads. Then a Viking band with horned helmets attacked us."

Alfred groaned. "How did they find my secret camp?"

It'll be common knowledge in the future's history books, thought Pat. *The F.B.I. must've looked it up and told their bull-kings exactly where to go.* "Sire," he said, "is there anywhere else we can go to recover your forces and decide what to do next?"

Alfred shook his head. "Our best hope would be to hide in the forest, but how can we when—"

He broke off at the sound of heavy clattering from the trees. Suddenly four bull-kings burst from the undergrowth and fanned out, surrounding Alfred's party. Pat gawked in amazement at the sight of their horses – patterned black and white, each boasted a pair of cow horns and a swollen udder!

"Surrender," growled the biggest bull-king, driving his cow-horse faster. The other bull-kings followed suit, tightening their circle around Pat and the men so there was no way out. "Surrender to our power!"

Pat was so afraid he thought he might poo himself! Then he realized *that* might not be such a bad idea . . .

While Alfred and his men were busy looking for a gap in the circling horses, Pat bent over and popped out a cowpat. One of the mutant horses stepped in it and slipped with a horrified *neigh*! *THUMP!* It landed on its side and threw its rider through the air. *BOINK!* The horns growing through his helmet jabbed into the

bottom of the horse in front of him,
giving the animal such a shock it reared
up and hurled its own rider backwards.
With a yell, the bull-king collided with
the one behind him and both fell in the
remains of Pat's whiffy parcel.

"The way out is clear!" cried Alfred
triumphantly. "Flee quickly, my subjects.

Pat and I shall lead our enemies away."

Pat had already clambered onto his long-suffering stallion. He rode up to the remaining bull-king, who was looking around in puzzled alarm, and shoved him off his mount. Then Alfred steered his horse towards the oak trees on the far side of the valley, and Pat did the same.

But already, the bull-kings were picking themselves up and readying their horses to follow ...

McMoo's mind was racing. Gaur had unstrapped him, but poor Bo still lay helpless on the booby-trapped stretcher. With Bo's life at stake, McMoo had had no choice but to do as the mad doctor demanded.

Gaur peered at McMoo through his extra-thick glasses. "The problem is, Professor, that something in the human body resists my moo-goo. The bull-kings who attacked you on the beach should have been much more cowish than they are."

"Then I'd better get studying a pure human, hadn't I?" suggested McMoo. "I suppose you've already fed moo-goo to those men Mookow brought you. What a good job you've still got Gruntbag and Henmir!"

Gaur stomped over to a control panel in one corner with a large red microphone and pressed a button. "Cow-lions, bring me that feeble pair you are guarding . . ."

"I'll just give Bo's ringblender back to her," said McMoo airily. "Don't want to confuse those Vikings before we experiment on them, eh?" He slid the silver ring back into his friend's nose, then tried discreetly to unplug the booby-trap cable. *ZAP!* A blast of electric energy sent him crashing to the floor.

"Prof!" cried Bo.

Gaur spun round and chuckled with evil satisfaction. "Ha! Did I forget to tell you I had booby-trapped my  booby-trap? What a shame!" He put in a ringblender of his own. "Now, do not try to trick me again or else!"

Just then, the entrance to the laboratory slid open to reveal two slavering cow-lions and two very frightened Vikings.

"Angus," Gruntbag wailed. "Is all this some terrible nightmare? I'll wager Odin himself has never seen such madness in all his reign."

"Rain!" McMoo clapped his hooves and turned to Gaur. "That's it! I'll bet Mookow's cloud rained all over the Vikings he captured, didn't it?"

"Yes," came a grating mechanical voice as

Mookow strode into the room. "My rain disarmed the human fools and caused chaos, allowing me to capture them."

"Ah, there you are, Mookow," said Gaur. "Have you caught Alfred the Great yet?"

"The power of my cloud has disabled his fort at Athelney and scattered his forces far and wide," Mookow announced proudly. "But bull-kings report that Alfred is being protected by a young warrior."

"It must be Pat!" cheered Bo. "Way to go, little bruv!"

"It is only a matter of time before both Alfred and Pat Vine are in my power," grated Mookow. "I have ordered all bull-kings to join the hunt."

"I should hope so too," said Gaur fussily. "Now, why were you going on about the rain, McMoo?"

The professor shrugged. "Perhaps some of the toxic chemicals in that water were

absorbed by their puny human bodies, and *that's* why they're resisting your moo-goo."

"It is possible . . ." Gaur turned on Mookow. "We need rain samples."

"Very well," Mookow growled reluctantly. He produced a white remote control from inside his tunic and carefully changed the settings, while Gaur busied himself gathering beakers.

Gruntbag and Henmir looked at McMoo in disbelief, and there was no mistaking the disappointment in Bo's eyes. "You're *really* going to help them?"

"I have to," McMoo said quietly. "With so much at stake, believe me – I have to!"

★

"I've got to rest," Pat panted, leaning against a tree somewhere in the Wessex woods.

"Very well," said King Alfred, short of breath himself. "But only for a few moments."

The two fugitives had ridden their horses for miles with the bull-kings close behind, until they came to a wide river. Abandoning their mounts, they had swum to the other side, and then continued on foot and hoof. Several times they had to dodge patrols of real Vikings, busy raiding monasteries or looting villages. Pat, like Alfred, longed to do something to stop them. But with the bull-kings on their trail, staying one step ahead had to be their priority.

"I wonder where we are?" said Pat.

"I'm not sure," Alfred admitted, his nose twitching. "But I can smell cooking."

Pat sniffed. The smell of fresh bread was faint in the air. He followed the smell to a clearing, where a simple peasant hut stood, smoke curling out of its single window. "This way, sire!" he hissed. Pat was quite fond of a bun or three, and the grass around here looked pretty juicy too. "We could use some food for extra energy."

"The rain melted my money," said Alfred.

"But you're king," Pat argued. "Anyone will give you bread."

"I dare not reveal who I really am," replied Alfred. "If the bull-kings learn I was here, they might torture the peasant folk for information leading to my capture."

"Then it's time to turn on the old Patrick charm," said Pat with a wink at Alfred. He strolled up to the door and knocked politely, preparing to turn his biggest, brightest grin on whoever answered.

But then the door opened to reveal a huge, lumbering woman in a stained smock, and his smile twisted into a horrified grimace. The woman was the very image of the Farmyard Queen of Cruelty – Bessie Barmer!

Chapter Nine

TRAPPED!

"What do you want?" the woman demanded, her chubby cheeks flushed red with heat, her hair a messy tangle.

Pat tried to rearrange his smile. "Um ...Your name wouldn't be Barmer, would it?"

"Nessie Barmer, as it happens." The dough-faced woman narrowed her eyes suspiciously. "How would you be knowing that?"

Pat gulped and thought fast. "Er ... You're quite famous in these parts for your amazing cooking. We'd love to try some ...Any chance of a free sample?"

"Cheek!" Nessie scowled. "If you want

any grub, you'll have to earn it. I haven't done any washing for two months – I could do with popping down to the stream to give my underclothes a good scrub. But I don't like to go out alone when those nasty Vikings are pillaging all over the place." She plumped up her rats'-maze hair. "Anything could happen to a good-looking girl like me, don't you think?"

"No," said Alfred. "But my friend will go with you, if I can shelter in your hut."

"Why me?" hissed Pat.

"Because I'm king," Alfred hissed back.

Nessie disappeared into her hut, then reappeared a few moments later with a massive bundle of clothes. "You can stay," she told Alfred, "but I've got some more cakes cooking. Make sure you take them out before they burn. Got it?"

Alfred nodded. "Many thanks, good lady."

"Come on then, boy!" Nessie gave Pat a shove. "Let's get going!"

Sighing wearily, Pat followed her.

* * *

Back at the F.B.I. undersea laboratory, McMoo, Bo and their Viking friends watched as Mookow's cloud came drifting through the ceiling and hovered above their heads.

"How can it pass through all that water above us without falling apart?" Bo wondered aloud.

"The cloud is made of a chemical gas that repels rain and seawater," Mookow replied proudly.

"And since you can steer it by remote control, I suppose it must be full of tiny electronic receivers that hold it in shape." McMoo beamed. "Isn't future technology wonderful?"

"No," said Gruntbag, and Henmir nodded with feeling.

Mookow held a plastic bucket under the cloud then pressed another button

on his remote control. The cloud obligingly squeezed out a little of the metal-eating liquid. Mookow held up the bucket to Gaur, who added a few drops from his test tube of moo-goo. "Now, let us see if one reacts badly to the other."

116

Sure enough, the liquid began to fizz and make a smell like rotting cabbage.

"It seems you are correct, Professor." Gaur narrowed his eyes at Mookow. "You should have tested your metal-eating chemicals on my moo-goo before using it."

Mookow glared back at him. "You should have tested your moo-goo on my metal-eating chemicals before using *it*."

"Don't argue, fellas!" McMoo rushed over to stand between them. "We found the problem, now all we need to do is work out which chemicals aren't getting on and sort them out." He pointed to a grey gadget the size and shape of a toaster with a screen on top. "Hey, isn't that a chemical analyser? That will tell me the exact ingredients of both your inventions. Make things way simpler! Let's get started, shall we?"

The professor snatched the test tube from Gaur and poured it into the analyser. A list of chemicals appeared on its screen, and he studied them intently.

"Interesting," he murmured. "*Very* interesting . . ."

Pat stood beside a stream with Nessie Barmer while she did her washing. She hummed loudly and tunelessly as she plunged dirty clothes into the water and then stamped on them. "Make yourself useful, boy," she growled at Pat. "Fold them up in a nice neat pile."

Grumbling, Pat picked up a skirt as big as a tablecloth – and as he did so, he thought he caught a glimpse of movement from the trees on the other side of the stream. Was he imagining things?

Crack! A stick broke loudly in the thicket ahead of them. A flash of steel and cowhide passed between two trees.

And then a bull-king pushed out of hiding!

"It's a Dane!" Nessie screamed, and the warrior covered his ears. Thinking fast, Pat hurled Nessie's skirt at the approaching bull-king. With a wet slap, the coarse material engulfed the menacing figure, who staggered back into the thick foliage.

"Come on!" Pat grabbed Nessie by her chunky elbow and hauled her away. "We must warn Alfred."

Pat raced back towards Nessie's hut, the big woman panting and wheezing behind him. Finally they reached the clearing – only to find thick black smoke pouring out of the window.

"I don't believe it!" snarled Nessie. "Your stupid friend has let my cakes burn!"

As the big woman pounded up to the hut, Pat suddenly remembered Professor McMoo recounting the story of how Alfred burned a peasant woman's cakes. "This is history as it happened," he breathed. "Typical that the peasant woman should be one of Bessie Barmer's relatives!"

Nessie kicked open the door and strode inside. "How dare you!" She booted

Alfred outside, and he yelped as he fell sprawling on the ground. A moment later she followed him out with a stone tray full of burned and blackened buns. "All you had to do was sit there and take my lovely cakes out when they were ready. Couldn't be bothered, could you?"

Alfred scrambled up. "Actually, I was busy thinking how to save the kingdom from villainous man-bull invaders!"

"Well, I hope you thought of something," said Pat, "because those evil invaders are on their way!"

Right on cue, Arlik the Mighty crashed into the clearing. At the sight of Alfred and Pat, he mooed menacingly and raised a huge battleaxe above his head. Pat and Alfred got ready to fight . . .

But then Nessie shoved them aside. "Don't mess with me in this mood, Sunbeam!" So saying, she chucked a still-smoking cake at the murderous man-monster. With incredible accuracy and a tooth-breaking crack, it struck Arlik in the mouth. The big man choked and clutched at his throat before collapsing. Pat turned to look at her in wonder. "Wow, Nessie – good shot!"

But then two more bull-kings lurched out from the cover of the trees. One had a sword, and the other had a bow and arrows. Even now the transmogrified archer was pulling back the drawstring, aiming at Alfred . . .

"Take cover!" Pat shoved Alfred back into Nessie's hut – just as an arrow thudded into the wall. Nessie screeched as more arrows came whizzing towards them. Pat dragged her inside the smoky building too, then slammed the door shut.

"We've had it now," said Alfred, watching as more bull-kings appeared from the woods and spread out to circle the hut. "We've got no weapons, and nowhere to run. They've got us trapped!"

McMoo was still working out the complicated mix of chemicals that went into a portion of moo-goo and metal-rain, when a barked command from Gaur distracted him: "Stop your muttering!"

He looked over his shoulder and saw Bo on the stretcher, wide-eyed and innocent, while Gruntbag stood beside her with a decidedly shifty expression on his face. *I wonder what they're up to*, he thought.

Just then, a loud beep came from the control panel with the microphone beside it. McMoo observed there were several red buttons built into the console, each one of them labelled: OCTOPUS, LIONS, TURTLES, ALL ANIMALS ... *Those controls must allow Gaur to give separate commands to each of his moo-gooed minions*, he realized. Right now, the button marked ARLIK was flashing.

Mookow pressed the button. "Report, Arlik."

"This is bull-king Group Alpha," came the jerky voice of the zombified Dane. "We have captured King Alfred and the C.I.A. agent Pat Vine. They report that further Vikings are hiding in a cave on the beach where Alfred was first sighted."

"Proceed there at once with your captives," Mookow told him. "I shall order all other bull-kings to that beach to capture the concealed Danes. We shall collect the whole lot of you from there shortly. That is all."

"Oh, my poor men!" sobbed Gruntbag, while Henmir sucked his thumb.

"And my poor little bruv!" Bo groaned. "At least while he was free we stood a chance of being rescued."

"Instead, I have another hostage to use against you, McMoo." Gaur giggled nastily. "You are all completely in my power. Nothing can stop the F.B.I. now! *Nothing!*"

Chapter Ten

EMOO-GENCY!

Struggling against her straps, Bo watched as McMoo toiled under the watchful stares of Mookow and Gaur, mixing chemicals in different beakers and nodding. She knew he was only helping the F.B.I. for the sake of his friends, but he really seemed to be getting into it.

If only I wasn't strapped down flat on my back, she thought miserably.

She had told Gruntbag to give a special instruction to Henmir, but the little Viking was so short she couldn't see from here whether or not he had done as she'd asked.

"Nearly there," the professor remarked.

Bo sighed. "You'll probably finish before Pat even arrives."

"He will still be useful as a hostage," said Gaur, peering at her through his huge glasses. "With the professor's help I will be able to create armies of bull-kings in half the time I'd imagined."

"Arlik's squad will soon be reaching the beach," droned Mookow. "Are the subjects I brought you this morning ready to fight?"

"I've fed them their moo-goo," Gaur said huffily. "But since they've been drenched by your silly old rain, the physical change will hardly be noticeable."

"Like it wasn't in Sven," McMoo noted.

Gaur turned
to his special
microphone
and pressed
a new, as yet
unmarked
button. "Bull-
king Squad
Delta, activate!"

A few seconds later, a door in the
far side of the lab slid open and Alfred's
men lurched inside. They were barely
recognizable – eyes blank, skin white
and leathery. Only the smallest of horns
were peeping through their special war
helmets, but each of the men was armed
with a gleaming sword or axe made of
chemical-proof modern metal.

Bo saw Gruntbag staring in horror
as the men filed through in silence, led
by big, bald Bryce, heading towards
the airlock and its supply of longships.
"That's the fate in store for us, Henmir!"

"Right about now, I'm afraid," said McMoo, holding up a large bowl of silvery-looking water. "Mookow, your super cloud needs to absorb this new mix of chemicals. Then it can melt any amount of metal without interfering with the full effect of the moo-goo."

"I do not trust you," grated Mookow.

McMoo crossed to Gruntbag and yanked away the chain he wore around his neck. Then he dropped it in the bowl and it sizzled away to nothing. "There you go. Even more potent than before."

Gaur gave one of his trademark titters. "Reload the cloud, Mookow," he cried. "Soak these puny Vikings, and then I'll feed them a few tasty mouthfuls of moo-goo. They'll never be the same."

"Professor!" Bo called. "You can't let them do this!"

"I'm afraid I must," said McMoo sadly.

Struggling still harder to be free, Bo watched as Mookow pressed his remote and the cloud slowly floated down from the ceiling. It hovered over the bowl and glowed brilliant white as it sucked up the silvery substance into its metal-mashing molecules. Bo closed her eyes against the blinding light . . .

Then, suddenly, she heard a shout from Henmir and a squeaky flapping noise.

With a surge of excitement, she opened her eyes to find the little Viking zooming about the room like a deranged parrot – wearing the professor's battered mechanical wings! Henmir thumped into Mookow and sent the ter-moo-nator staggering into Gaur. Together they crashed into the lab bench and fell in a heap, while the tiny Dane flapped on in a crazy circle.

"You did it, Henmir!" Bo shouted. "You sneaked into the magic wings, just as I told you!"

"Being so small, no one noticed him slipping them on!" said Gruntbag proudly.

"I wish they had!" said McMoo crossly.

"But it's a fab distraction," Bo argued. "Gaur told us the wings wouldn't hold *our* weight, but they can still support a pint-sized Viking. Now quick, get me off this electric stretcher so we can all escape."

But just then, Henmir swooped down and smashed into the booby-trapped wire. There was a flash of sparks as the wire snapped and the wings blew apart, flinging the little man to the floor.

"Oh, Henmir," groaned McMoo, rushing over to check he was OK. "If only you'd held off for just a few moments longer . . ."

"Attention, cow-lions!" A furious Gaur

had pulled himself up by his microphone. "Return to the lab at once. Eat the girl and the two puny Vikings!"

"No!" McMoo shouted. "Bo didn't mean to cause trouble."

"I flipping did!" Bo retorted.

"And I won't help you if you hurt the three of them," McMoo went on quickly.

Mookow was back on his mechanical feet. "You have no choice. Remember, Pat Vine is in our power. He will take their place as hostage."

Suddenly the main door slid open and the two cow-lions pounced inside.

"Uh-oh." McMoo grabbed some scissors from the table and sliced through Bo's straps. "Time to get *moo*-ving!"

Gruntbag helped Bo roll off and stood protectively in front of her. "Foul freaks of nature," he cried, "eat me first!"

"Or better yet, try a mouthful of stretcher!" As the fearsome beasts advanced, McMoo tipped the trolley on

top of them
and pinned
the cow-
lions to the
ground.
He
flashed
a quick grin at
Gruntbag. "Couldn't
let you get eaten after acting as brave as
that, could I?"

"Me, brave? I . . . I suppose I was." The
Viking beamed. "I never knew I had it in
me!"

"You'll have a cow-lion's *teeth* in you
if we don't hurry!" McMoo used the
upturned trolley as a springboard to leap
out through the exit. "Bring Henmir and
come on!"

Bo wrapped her blanket around her,
kissed Gruntbag on the cheek, then
grabbed the dazed Henmir and hauled
him from the lab.

McMoo was waiting for them outside, and the moment they were through he hit the door control. The heavy shutter slid down a split-second before Gaur and Mookow reached it. *THUMP! WHUMP!*

Bo chuckled at the sound of the F.B.I. agents slamming into the barrier. "Cool – we're free!"

"But Pat isn't," McMoo reminded her, helping Henmir to his dinky feet. "Those two creeps can still use him against us."

"And their bull-kings will be after my crew in the cave," Gruntbag added.

McMoo picked up Henmir. "We must

follow Alfred's brainwashed men to the airlock and get to the beach as fast as we can."

"You'll never make it," Gaur warned them from behind the door. "I will send *all* my animals to get you!"

"Sounds like things could get messy." Bo shoved Gruntbag down the corridor ahead of her. "Follow that professor!"

McMoo put Henmir down and peered out from behind the airlock's door as the F.B.I.'s newest recruits clambered clumsily into a longship.

Frantic footfalls behind signalled the arrival of Bo and Gruntbag. "OK, Professor," Bo panted, "how do we get out of here?"

"The bull-kings are under Gaur's control. They don't seem to have thoughts of their own. So until they're told to deal with us, they shouldn't take any notice if we sneak on board."

Carefully, McMoo crept over to the Viking vessel and climbed inside. Still dazed, Henmir let Gruntbag carry him like hand luggage and stow him in the ship beside the professor. Then he and Bo climbed inside too. The bull-kings did not turn round and apparently hadn't noticed a thing, sitting in stupefied silence.

Shortly, two of the massive cow-turtles waddled up and stood at each end of the vessel. Both blew the same sort of thick rubbery bubble as the oxtopus. The two bubbles met in the middle and completely covered the longship. Seawater gushed out at high speed from the drain in the floor, and the big yellow bubble began to float, like the mother of all rubber ducks.

McMoo gave Bo's hoof a comforting squeeze. "That hatchway above should open at any moment . . ."

Even as
he spoke,
the white
plastic roof
slid open
to reveal
the waiting
oxtopus, its
thick fleshy
tentacles
reaching in
to grab the
giant bubble.
McMoo gasped
as they were propelled swiftly through
the dark waters until they bobbed into
daylight on the sea's surface. The oxtopus
squeezed tight and the bubble burst,
leaving them safe and dry. As one, the
bull-kings started to row for shore with
strong, powerful strokes.

"What do we do when we reach the
beach?" asked Bo quietly. "Gaur said

he was going to send his mad mooing animals after us."

"And if we are going to save Pat and Alfred we'll have to fight their captors," mused McMoo. "Not to mention this boatload of zombies. I'm afraid, Gruntbag, that if your men wish to remain free, they must fight."

"And fight we shall," squeaked Henmir.

Gruntbag nodded grimly. "I've had a yellow-bellyful of being a coward!"

But suddenly the waters churned and foamed behind them as Gruntbag's own ship broke the surface of the Bristol Channel in another bubble. Gaur, Mookow and a mad menagerie of moo-gooed animals were sitting inside. The moo-nkey beat its black and white chest. The e-moo flapped its leathery wings. The strange skunk raised its tail and the cow-ponies reared up beside the savage lion-beasts.

Gaur's voice carried as he spoke into a futuristic walkie-talkie. "Attention, my bull-kings," he yelled. "There are enemies right behind you. Capture the biggest one — and kill the rest!"

Slowly the zombified crew turned as one to stare at their stowaways . . .

Chapter Eleven

HARD RAIN

"I think it's time to split!" Bo jumped up and tail-whipped the nearest bull-king, knocking him off his seat. Then she grabbed his oar and tucked it between her legs like a witch's broomstick. "Better jump on in front of me, guys – *oar* else!"

With more bull-kings already gearing up to attack them, McMoo and Gruntbag did as

she suggested, and Henmir scrambled up onto McMoo's shoulders. As the big bald man and the archer lunged for them, the desperate stowaways jumped ship and splashed down in the water, riding the oar.

"Hang on!" Bo shouted. Wriggling around in the water to face the other way, she lifted her blanket and squirted a super-powerful jet of milk from her udder. It worked like an outboard motor, the milk stream pushing them onward across the sea towards the shore.

Gruntbag clung onto the oar for all he was worth. "We're going forward without rowing. How can that be?"

"You really don't want to know," McMoo assured him.

Bo kept up the milky thrust until she

was udderly exhausted – but by then, they were close enough to the beach to swim the rest of the way. McMoo checked behind him. The bull-kings' longship wasn't far behind. And with Mookow rowing his mechanical socks off, Gaur and his animals were gaining fast too.

Bo was first to reach dry land, and she helped Gruntbag and Henmir out of the water. Ivar peered timidly from the nearby cave. "You're back! You've been gone a whole day!"

"And we've brought trouble," said Gruntbag breathlessly. "Our enemies are on our tail and if we don't fight, they will kill us all."

Ivar's face fell as he looked out to sea. "Couldn't we just run away?"

"Not this time," said McMoo, pointing both ways along the beach. "Look."

Ivar saw that groups of bull-kings on

horseback were approaching from both directions. "Halfdan the Hole-puncher to our left . . . Karl the Crusher to our right . . ."

Bo pointed up at the cliff top. "And Arlik and his men are blocking the only other way out of here. They've got Pat and King Alfred as their prisoners!"

"Here come the bull-kings to chop us into pieces," Gruntbag cried as the longship scraped up on to the beach. "With Gaur and Mookow and all their killer cow-beasts right behind them."

"Quickly, Ivar," said McMoo. "It's time

to get out that trunk full of weapons.
And fetch Sven too — we must bring him
out in the open, it's important."

"Right!" Henmir declared. "We may
be outnumbered at least ten to one and
facing a dreadful death, but we'll go out
smiling, eh, lads?"

"No," chorused Ivar and the other
Vikings. But slowly, dragging their chest,
they emerged into the daylight.

Gruntbag ducked into the cave and pulled out the still-sleeping Sven; the skinny Viking's horns had grown longer and his skin was more cow-like than before.

"It's no good, Professor." Bo pointed out to sea, where a familiar fluffy shape was forming. "Mookow's brought his cloud with him. Now you've improved his formula he'll melt Gruntbag's weapons faster than ever."

"I'm hoping he'll try to," said McMoo, eyes agleam with excitement.

"Professor! Bo!" Pat cried from halfway down the cliff side, Arlik's big hands gripping his shoulders. "Are you all right?"

Bo nodded bravely as Bryce led his fellow bull-kings onto the beach. "Nothing we like better than a fight against impossible odds!"

Alfred, clamped in the grip of Sam the Scar-maker, stared at the unfolding scene in horror. "Bryce, no!" he yelled. "You're an Anglo-Saxon, not a bull . . . We must band together and fight our real enemies!"

But now Gaur and Mookow's ship had run up onto the beach, the snarls and snorts of the angry cow-animals drowning out the sea's roar.

"We're cut off on all sides!" wailed Ivar.

"We will show you the meaning of *cut off*," droned Mookow, raising his battleaxe.

Gaur nodded. "Bull-kings, animals . . . ATTACK!"

At the snarled command, Bryce's bull-kings advanced, and the moo-gooed animals splashed through the shallow water to join them on the beach. Bo grabbed a sword from the chest, and Gruntbag quickly passed the rest of the weapons around his men. As the forces of evil closed in, McMoo gave Mookow and Gaur a defiant smile.

But suddenly Pat yelled out from the cliff side, "If we'd known you were all coming, we'd have baked a cake." He pulled a charred black bun from inside his tunic. "Oh, hang on a sec — we did!"

"Indeed we did," Alfred agreed, pulling two more buns from behind his back.

"And we intend to use them." Arlik let go of his 'prisoners' to pull a whole handful of buns out from inside his breeches.

"What are you lot on about?" called Bo, frowning as Bryce, the animals and the other bull-kings kept up their steady advance. "This is no time for cakes – especially ones that look as horrible as that."

"Oh yes it is," Pat corrected her. "It's time for us to—"

"*Open fire!*" bellowed King Alfred. He hurled his buns, and so did Pat. Arlik tossed a cake to Sam the Scar-maker and joined in the strange attack. The rock-hard missiles struck Bryce and the others around the face and shoulders.

Ivar stared. "Vikings and English fighting together?"

"Rubbish shots, the lot of you," came a booming, high-pitched voice from the cliff top.

Bo looked up in amazement to see a wobbly, wild-haired woman with a whole bag of cakes at her side. "It's another of Bessie's ancestors!"

"Trust Pat to sniff out one of those!" McMoo marvelled as the woman chucked her cakes with incredible accuracy, landing one right inside Bryce's mouth and another in the gob of Halfdan the Hole-puncher. "Not bad, is she?"

"Fools!" shouted Gaur. "You think you can stop my warrior slaves with baking?"

"They already stopped *me*," thundered Arlik. "Nessie's burned buns are so truly revolting, they shocked me back to my senses!"

"Must be the memory of eating human food that reminded them they aren't bulls," McMoo realized. "Combined with a taste so yukky, neither human *nor* cow could ever stomach it!"

Pat nodded cheerily. "So, when we saw the cake had broken the spell over Arlik, we shoved them in the mouths of his attacking friends, too," he called down. "When they awoke and saw the horrible things Mookow and Gaur had done to them, they agreed to join us and help awaken the rest of their warriors."

"So when Arlik called Mookow, it was a trick," Bo exclaimed with delight.

"It was Pat's idea," Alfred agreed, smiling as Bryce spat out what was left of the cake and looked around in confusion. "He got Arlik to mention Gruntbag's crew as a way to lure those wicked magicians out of hiding. And once we've broken the spell placed on the rest of our men, we shall avenge ourselves!"

"Enough talk," boomed Arlik as he raised his sword and charged down to

the shore. "FIIIIIIIIIIIIIIIIIGHT!"

Mookow led the bull-kings to meet Arlik's charge . . .

And the beach became a battlefield.

Arlik and Sam tore into the ter-moo-nator, but he met their blows and got in several of his own. Alfred dragged the dazed and baffled Bryce clear, snatched the man's weapon and threw himself into the fray. Despite Nessie's skilful bun bombardment there were still many brainwashed bull-kings under F.B.I. control — and they began to attack Gruntbag and his men without pity. Bo dodged a leaping cow-lion, and only just managed to block an axe-blow from Karl the Crusher. The e-moo threw itself at the professor, whacking him with its impressive udder while pecking him on the head. Cow-horses reared up and tried to trample anyone who got in their way. Even the cow-turtles got in on the act, nipping at Pat's ankles while he tried to force a bun into a bull-king archer's mouth. The landscape echoed with the clang of swords and axes, the screaming roars of wild moo-tants and the thump of horrid buns on hides and heads.

"Good work, my friends!" McMoo flipped the giant cow-bird on top of a turtle and raised his voice. "I only hope Mookow doesn't send his raincloud to get us — that would be a disaster! Dearie me, yes! We'll be finished for sure if he does . . ."

"The C.I.A. fool's quite correct, Mookow!" cried Gaur, hopping up and down on the shore. "Melt their metal — once they've lost their weapons, we'll really have them at our mercy!"

Bo groaned. "You and your big mouth, Professor! What have you done?"

"We'll soon see." McMoo butted a cow-lion into Karl the Crusher — and saw the ter–moo–nator switch on his white remote control. "Stand by for a drenching, everybody!"

"Oh, no!" Looking out to sea, Gruntbag saw the cloud hurtling towards the shore. "Here it comes!"

Bo made a grab for Mookow's remote but missed – and a cow-lion brought her down. She struggled with it, fighting to keep its jaws from her throat. But then Pat made it through the battling throng and conked the lion on the head. He helped Bo up and gave her a hug – as the cloud burst open with its chemical rain.

"We are doomed!" Alfred cried. His sword began to melt in the downpour. Gruntbag groaned as his sword too disappeared in silver dribbles. Mookow laughed to see the Vikings' dismay as their weapons withered away.

"We don't need to collect Gruntbag's grotty Vikings," Gaur sneered, drawing closer despite the rain. "Kill them. Along with the C.I.A. girl."

"No!" cried Pat.

"Yes," hissed Mookow. He and the remaining bull-kings stomped closer.

"Come on," McMoo muttered. "Come on, come on, come on . . ."

Mookow raised his battleaxe high above his head, ready to strike Bo and Gruntbag in a single slaughtering stroke . . .

Chapter Twelve

SPLASHING OUT

Bo braced herself for the end . . .

But suddenly Mookow's axe started dripping silver rivulets! "Impossible," the ter-moo-nator grated, gazing at the melting metal. "Bull-kings' weapons are made from future alloys. They cannot be affected by my chemical rain."

"Ah, but it isn't *your* rain any longer, is it? You let *me* near it." McMoo snatched the white remote control from Mookow's hoof and grinned triumphantly. "I thought I'd mix in some *extra* chemicals. The stuff still works on old metal, but now it dissolves future metal too!"

Bo beamed as the bull-kings blundered

about, their helmets running into their eyes. "So that's what you were up to in the laboratory!"

"Turn it off! Make it stop!" Gaur ran out of the rain but the damage had been done – the frames of his glasses were melting and the lenses fell to the ground. "I can't see a thing. Help, Mookow!"

But Mookow was having an even worse time of it. "Components dissolving," he warbled through a mouthful of molten metal. "Systems shutting down. Escape to the twenty-sixth century imperative."

"You're a genius, Professor," Pat cheered.

McMoo nodded. "True!"

Nessie Barmer lumbered up, red-faced from running down the cliff side, and surveyed the scene. "Well," she declared, "if that doesn't take the cake!"

"Our enemies are beaten," yelled Alfred, tripping up a bull-king and shoving a blackened bun in his mouth. "Their magic is turned against them."

"Who needs weapons anyway?" Arlik flung down the mushy remains of his bull-king sword. "I'll smash those mad magicians with my bare hands . . ."

"Mission abort!" Staggering out of the rain, Mookow pulled a silver disc from beneath the bubbling armour on his back and threw it down onto the sand. "Quickly, before the portable time machine melts too."

"Wait for me!" Gaur rolled onto the platter, and in a haze of black smoke the pitiful pair disappeared.

"More magic?" Gruntbag shook his head in wonder.

Ivar slapped a hand down on his leader's shoulder. "The real magic is that we finally found our courage. We stood up to those horrors."

"And we won!" chirped Henmir.

"*And* we're all getting soaked," Alfred complained.

"Don't knock it, sire!" McMoo chuckled and studied the remote. "I'll see if I can turn it off." But the cloud's remote control couldn't stand up to the rain either. It smoked and sizzled. Then the cloud itself began to flash as if lightning were trapped inside its cotton-wool contours. A few moments later it blasted itself apart, leaving nothing but a thick fog in the air.

"Hey, Prof," said Bo. "I just had a thought. Our ringblenders are metal, aren't they?"

Pat gulped. "And after all that rain—"

The three C.I.A. agents gasped as the silver rings in their snouts dripped away on to the sand. "Back to being cattle again," murmured McMoo. "Quick, take off those human outfits before anyone sees us . . ."

When the fog cleared a minute or so later, Alfred, Gruntbag and the rest were surprised to find that the professor, Pat and Bo had vanished.

"What happened?" Henmir wondered. "Where did they go?"

"Perhaps they faded into the air, like the magicians," said Alfred quietly. "But they shall always be remembered as true heroes."

"Hey, look." Ivar pointed to a sleeping lion and a confused-looking turtle. "Their cow markings are fading. They are ordinary animals again!"

"So are the horses," Nessie realized. "And the big, horrible bird thing." The former e-moo pecked her bum. "OW!"

"Never mind the animals, look at Sven!" Gruntbag's grin was a half-mile wide. "He's getting back to normal."

"So too are my brothers of the sea," said Arlik with satisfaction.

Slowly Sven stirred and scratched his head. As he did so, his horns crumbled away like wet chalk. "I don't remember a thing," he groaned. "What happened?"

Gruntbag embraced him, and the rest of his crew piled in for a group hug. "A miracle happened!"

"Or a *moo*-racle at least," said Alfred, clapping Bryce on the back as the big man's own horns fell away. Then he turned to Arlik and his Vikings. "Danes, there has been much fighting today – and for once, both our sides have won. Let us call a truce for now, and do battle again some other day."

Arlik nodded slowly. "Very well. I confess I have a terrible headache after losing my horns – and a terrible tummy-ache from those buns!" Then he turned to Gruntbag. "You know, I always thought you and your band were puny and useless. But with my own eyes, I have seen you fight today like true warriors. I am proud to call you and your men my brothers."

The skinny Vikings cheered, and Gruntbag glowed with pride. "Thanks, Arlik. Although I think the life of farmers back in the northern lands would suit us better."

"Hang on a minute," said Nessie slowly, looking at Alfred. "You're . . . the *king*?"

"You catch on fast, madam," said Alfred, amused. "And I seem to recall you kicked my royal butt . . ."

Nessie gulped and hurried away. "Umm, the life of a farmer in the northern lands sounds good to me too. Bye!"

"Well, I hope she makes a better job of farming in *this* century than she does in ours," murmured Bo. She, Pat and McMoo

had rushed off to hide in the same cave that had sheltered the Vikings, and were peeking out at the scene taking place on the beach. "I'm glad everyone's friends now the F.B.I. have been sorted out. But how come the moo-goo wore off like that?"

"Well," said McMoo, "once I'd learned what moo-goo was made of, it was an easy job to muck up Mookow's rain even further to reverse the effect." He shrugged modestly. "Any incredibly brilliant genius could have done it."

"You really *are* brilliant, Professor," said Pat with a smile, watching as Alfred's men and the back-to-normal Vikings went their separate ways. Soon they were all out of sight. "Now all we have to do is get the C.I.A. to clean up Gaur and Mookow's mess — and go back home!"

"But the Time Shed is miles away!" Bo stuck out her tongue. "It'll take for ever to walk back there."

"Well, in that case . . ." McMoo smiled as a large white cube appeared on the beach in a purple haze of light, startling a skunk. "Perhaps we can hitch a lift with these guys?"

"A C.I.A. time machine!" Pat realized.

The cube grew solid and a door in one side slid open. A tough-looking black bull wearing shades and a purple sash stepped out onto the beach, followed by cows in white suits wielding big nets. One of the lions growled at him. The bull growled back, and the lion cowered away.

166

"Yakky-babes!" Bo squealed, running out of hiding and grabbing Yak in a clumsy hug. "How are you doing, Mr C.I.A. director, sir? Miss me?"

"No," Yak grumbled, trying to wriggle free of her embrace.

McMoo and Pat followed her onto the beach. "Hey, Yak," said McMoo. "What are you doing here already?"

"We picked up a very sorry pair of F.B.I. agents in our own time," Yak explained. "Mookow looked like a half-melted ter-moo-nator ice cream, and that mad scientist I've been chasing, Gaur, was bawling his eyes out because he couldn't see a thing. We said we'd only help them if they told us everything – and they did."

"So now you can take these poor animals back to their zoos in the twenty-sixth century," said Pat happily. "And dismantle the F.B.I.'s undersea base."

"What about that poor oxtopus?" asked Bo. "He's still guarding it."

"We'll make sure all the animals are back to normal," Yak assured her. "And as a way of saying thank you to my three best agents . . ."

"Yes?" said McMoo, Pat and Bo eagerly.

Yak grinned. "I'll even give you a lift back to the Time Shed!"

Director Yak was as good as his word, and it wasn't long before the Cows In Action were beside their ramshackle time machine once again.

"Oh, one more thing." Yak ducked back inside his cuboid craft and came out with a gift-wrapped bundle. "Prime *Moo*-ver Holstein asked me to give you this. He says it's to make up for something you lost."

"Cheers, Yak. Say thank you for me, won't you!" McMoo opened the shed's doors and ushered Pat and Bo inside. "See you next time."

Yak nodded. "*In* the next time!"

McMoo closed the doors, tossed the present to Bo and started flicking switches and twisting controls on the main console. "Right then! I'll set the controls to take us back to the farm just a few moments after we left." He pulled the take-off lever and the shed groaned and rattled as it began its journey back through the centuries. "Stick the kettle on, Pat, I'm spitting feathers . . ."

"And it looks like I'll be *wearing* them!" Bo had torn off the paper from the director's gift and proudly held up a new set of mechanical wings. "Holsty must have known I'd mashed up the old ones."

McMoo studied the wings. "Not bad," he admitted. "Not as good as mine, obviously, but worth trying out."

"Yes!" Bo quickly strapped them on. "It'll still be early on the farm. I can go

for a test flight straight away."

Pat passed the professor a steaming
bucket of tea, then smiled at his sister.

"And I've got a great idea for what you can do . . ." He whispered in Bo's ear.

"Oh, yes!" Bo clapped her hooves together in excitement as the Time Shed clanked back into the twenty-first century. "Gangway, Professor!" She charged out through the doors, pressed the button on her chest and took straight to the air, making for the Barmers' farmhouse.

Pat and McMoo drank their tea, then followed her outside. "What is she up to?" the professor wondered. "She'd better be careful. Look – Bessie Barmer's come to enjoy her view again."

"Not for long," Pat chuckled.

Bo hovered just above Bessie's bedroom windows – then released a flurry of cowpats all over the glass!

Bessie let out an enormous shriek. "What's going on? My beautiful view! What bird could do that?" Furiously she threw open the window and looked

outside – just in time to receive Bo's final cow pie right on her head! "Aaarrghhh!"

Giggling naughtily, Bo swooped down from the sky and landed beside Pat and the professor. "How did I do?"

"Not bad," Pat laughed. "Quick, let's get out of here before she sees us!"

"That was a top-class flight, Bo," said McMoo, leading the charge back to their field. "But, you know, wings or not, we'll always be high-flying agents of the C.I.A. – anyplace, anywhere and any time you can imagine!"

Visit www.**stevecolebooks**.co.uk for
fun, games, jokes, to meet the characters
and much, much more!

Welcome to a world where dinosaurs fly
spaceships and cows use a time-machine . . .

Sign up for the free Steve Cole monthly
newsletter to find out what your favourite
author is up to!

ALSO BY STEVE COLE

DINOSAURS...
IN SPACE!

**Meet Captain Teggs Stegosaur
and the crew of the amazing spaceship
DSS *Sauropod* as the ASTROSAURS fight
evil across the galaxy!**

IF YOU CAN'T TAKE THE SLIME
DON'T DO THE CRIME!

Plog, Furp, Zill and Danjo aren't just monsters in a rubbish dump. They are crime-busting super-monsters, here to save their whiffy world!